SURPRISE BABY FOR CHRISTMAS

A SECRET BABY ROMANCE

HARMONY KNIGHT

PIPPA

March 27, 2018

"**W**ait there."

Aiden's voice makes me look up from where I'm lying on the floor with a lazy smile on my face. I bite my lip on purpose, because even though we've only known each other for a week, I've already picked up on the little things that drive him wild. Lip biting is one of them. I see his eyes narrow on me, hungry, before he rushes out of the room.

I'm naked, lying on a fur rug that I hope is a fake, in front of a roaring open fire, inside a log cabin. When I gaze at the window, I can see the fire's reflection dancing over the scene outside. It's close to midnight and the moon is out, an almost-perfect circle suspended high over the mountains and trees below, its light glittering across the thick blanket of snow that covers them, pillowy and undisturbed.

I shouldn't be here, really. Vacations like this don't happen to girls like me—but they do happen to girls like

Valerie, my best friend. Where I turned to art and followed my passion right into borderline poverty, she followed hers into law school. The bad thing about being a lawyer only a couple of years out of college is that, if the boss says you have to cancel your vacation and come into work next week because there's a big client coming in, you have to ask how high. And then what do you do with your expensive, no-refunds, luxury ski break? Well, if you're an absolute treasure like Valerie, you offer it up to your poor sculptor bestie and loan her your gear.

I feel bad for her, but if I'd said no this whole thing would have gone to waste. And I'd never have met Aiden.

Just the thought of him sends a ripple of pleasure up my spine. We met at the lodge bar on the second night I was here, and it's just been one long whirlwind ever since. I can't let anything get too serious, not with such a recent break up hanging over my head. One in a string of many—I feel like I've barely been single since college. I've made it very clear that this is a vacation-only thing and we won't be swapping information, but I'd be lying if I said I wasn't tempted. I haven't asked Aiden about his job, his life at home... not even where he lives. Assuming, that is, he doesn't live here. When I arrived he was hanging out with the owner, and the first time we met he offered to teach me to ski, so I just figured that he worked here. But he's spent pretty much every evening with me since then, so I either got lucky and happened to be here when he had a week off, or he's on vaca-tion too. I guess I'll never know. He's respected my firm request that we just enjoy this week and then let it end, and hasn't asked anything about my life.

He returns waving a bottle of wine in one hand and two glasses in the other. "Got it," he smiles, walking toward me. "All I can tell you is that it's French, and old. Here, want to see the bottle?"

This man is drop-dead gorgeous. He is an adonis, and he really doesn't seem to realize it.

I prop up on one elbow to watch him walk over. He is toned like I've never seen. Michelangelo's David has nothing on this guy. His torso is broad at the top and narrow at the waist, his legs are sculpted from hip to foot. His stomach is a washboard complete with six bars of soap. His face? Perfection. Chiseled jaw, intense brown eyes, dark hair. If you'd told me about this guy a couple of weeks ago, I would have said there was no way in hell I could ever let someone that perfect see me naked, with all my wobbly imperfections. But here I am, and here he is. I think our vacation-only rule has made me throw caution to the wind. Who cares if he sees a little cellulite? After tomorrow, I'll never see him again. And yeah, maybe I wish he'd pushed back against my request for a no-strings fling a bit harder than he did, but it's really for the best, I'm sure.

"Well?" he says, standing over me in all his naked glory. He's holding the bottle by its neck and waving it back and forth, and it couldn't be more obvious that I can't even remember the question anymore. I've just been laying here, staring. I clear my throat.

"Sorry, what?" I ask.

A smile creeps onto his mouth, slow and seductive. "Like what you see?" he asks.

I look at the bottle and then at him, drawing my gaze down slowly over his whole, delicious body. I see his length twitch as I glance at it, a sure sign that it's about to get considerably lengthier. "Are we still talking about the wine?" I ask him.

He twitches again and begins to grow. The wine is forgotten. I don't see what happens to the bottle, but he is on top of me suddenly, his mouth on mine, his tongue seeking to dance with my own. I respond without hesitation. It might be the very last time, after all.

He shifts himself on top of me in a way that urges me to open my thighs, and I need no further encouragement to comply. His large hand moves to my right leg, pulling it up at the knee so I can hook it around his waist.

He's fully hard now. He grabs a condom from an open pack beside the rug and slips it on with ease. Then I can feel him pressing against my sex, not entering me but pushing through my wetness until he finds that sensitive little nub and rocks his hips, teasing me, earning himself a gasp from my mouth that seems to delight him. He smiles against my mouth, and then nibbles at my bottom lip. "I'm going to miss this," he says.

I thrust my hips a little, impatiently, only to moan as he slides over that sensitive little bud again. I try to ignore the sinking feeling at the reminder that this will all be over soon.

"Better make it memorable." My own voice is a stranger to me, husky and breathless. My nipples are almost as hard as he is, and he stimulates them with every pass as his body rocks that slow, teasing rhythm, still refusing to enter me, no matter how insistently I tug at him with that leg hooked around his waist.

"Ask for it," he whispers beside my ear, his breathing heavy, his voice low and demanding. I feel my cheeks flush pink and hot. I roll my hips, pulling my body against him, defying his demand, and watch his composure falter a little. His jaw tightens slightly. He looks me right in the eye and raises one brow, slowing the rhythmic motion of his hips.

The delicious ripples of pleasure that have been rolling through my body stop abruptly as he stills, and a smirk lifts one corner of his mouth. He knows as well as I do that this deprivation will break my playful resistance.

"Please," I say, leaning up to nibble quickly on his lower lip.

"Please, what?" he asks. The smirk is infuriating by now. I

can still feel the heat of his body radiating against me, almost as hot as the open fire beside us.

I curl my hands to fists in the fur beneath me, for a little leverage, and slide my hips up quickly, lining up his tip before quickly thrusting forward and pulling him toward me with the leg I have hooked around his waist.

"Ah-hah!" I grin, triumphantly, as he slides into me, but my triumph is short-lived. He narrows his eyes and pushes a little deeper, staring into me. A little deeper yet and my triumphant exclamation is drowned out by a groan of pleasure from my own lips. I feel him stretch me, and my body responds instantly, my other leg coming up so that both are wrapped around his waist.

His left hand pushes a stray hair out of my face, while his right moves down between my legs, between our bodies. He presses his thumb against that sensitive nub that he's already teased toward the edge, and I see that smirk return to his face.

"That was very naughty, Pip," he tells me, and sweeps his thumb up and back down. A shock of pleasure shoots through me and my body, pinned beneath him, twitches.

"Sorry," I whisper, breathless. "I don't know what I was thinking. I'm normally such a good girl."

He laughs. His laugh is gorgeous, masculine and unbridled, and it dies easy against my lips as he kisses me, and finally starts to fuck me, slowly at first, and then with every ounce of energy and enthusiasm he has. His thumb works overtime on my clitoris, rubbing gentle, small circles that match the rhythm of his hips. In barely a couple of minutes I am gasping, digging nails into his back, gripping at the fur rug beneath me, and arching my back as the pleasure builds.

His breathing is heavy. He slips his hand beneath my neck and holds me, pulling up a little as though to watch my face and all its many expressions as he pushes my body closer and closer to its limit.

"You're so fucking gorgeous," he tells me, through gritted teeth, as he struggles to hold on himself.

It doesn't even occur to me, with him, to object to the praise. He could tell me anything in this moment and I'd moan some superficial agreement. His hips thrust and roll a few more times, harder, and the sound of our bodies meeting is drowned out by my sudden gasp. I hold it as the pressure builds in my belly, and then all at once it comes flooding out. Wave after wave of pleasure rolls through my bucking body, and I moan with every one.

I can feel Aiden's eyes on me, intently, watching every millisecond of my orgasm play out on my flushed face and through my body. Just as I feel the pleasure begin to ebb away, he picks up the pace. He slams into me harder and faster, pushing his own limits and sending me off on the crest of another wave. I feel him tense, muscles bunching on his back and his shoulders as he slams into me one final time and holds, and I feel him pumping inside me as he groans loudly beside my ear.

"Jesus," he says, breathless, as he leans down and kisses my lips gently. He pulls out of me slowly and rolls off me. Laying beside me on the rug, he runs his fingers up and down my tummy, making me twitch and giggle in the super-sensitive afterglow. I'm a mess, but the way he looks at me makes me feel like a queen.

"Jesus," I whisper, smiling at him.

AIDEN

March 28, 2018

I'm awake before I open my eyes, feeling content and warm—if a bit hungover. I can already tell the room is bright from the sun's reflection off the snowy banks outside, and I can hear the faint crackle and pop of the dying fire. But as comfortable as I am, something feels off.

Reluctantly, I peel my eyes open and look around; first at the wooden beams splayed across the ceiling of the cabin, then towards the fire on my right, and finally, apprehensively, to my left. She's not there. No matter how hard I try to stop myself falling, no matter how much I remind myself that this is a temporary, week-long adventure and then it'll be over, I already feel like something's not quite right when she isn't beside me. At some point today she will leave, and I'll let her go without a single protest. Because I gave her my word that I would.

I sit up with a groan and rub my hands over my face, settle my elbows on my knees and try to clear the last remnants of wine from my head. I've just about convinced myself to get up when there's a knock at the door.

"It's open," I call, my voice cracking with residual sleep. It's always open. I've been coming to this same lodge twice a year since I was a boy. The people here are like family. I've been helping out teaching new skiers since I was fifteen, and occasionally working the bar since I was twenty-one. I spent a whole year here in my late teens. I'm pretty sure Pippa thinks I live and work here now, but the only time I did that was when I needed to take some time out from life, to let my heart mend for a while.

The door opens and Dave walks in, dressed in full snow gear with a smile on his face. "Morning!" he says, smiling. Behind him, disturbed flakes of snow flutter down from above the door.

It's at that moment that a blast of icy cold air hits my bare torso. "Holy shit, Dave! Close the door!" I pull the blanket up over my chest and he laughs.

"Where's Pip?" he asks, and I almost groan at the reminder that she's not here. In all the years he's known me, from my trips here to his parents' ski resort and his trips to Chicago to see me in the summer, he's never known me to spend as much time with a girl as I have with Pippa. Not since college, at least. My best friend asking me about her somehow makes her leaving much more real.

He must be able to read the conflict on my face, because the smile vanishes as he walks in and drops onto the couch. "Man, she's gone?" he says, picking up a piece of paper from the coffee table.

"Going," I say. "Today."

"Ah, yeah," he says, flapping the paper toward me. "At five. Did you give her your number?"

"Is that from her?" I ask, gripping the blanket around my waist as I lean forward to snatch the paper from his hand. It reads: *Gone to pack. Cab at 5. Meet at Driscoll's at 3? P. xoxo*

8

"Shit. What time is it?" I demand from Dave. I stand up to look for my phone, still holding the blanket around me like a makeshift sarong. I almost trip over it on my second step, and just manage to stop myself by gripping onto the mantel. "Jesus, my head," I groan.

Dave is wearing a half-amused expression as he watches me bumble around.

"Not even two," he says, putting me out of my misery.

"Right." Sighing with relief, I can feel my pulse slowing a little and I stand there, scratching my head.

"I'll make you a coffee and find some aspirin," Dave says, getting to his feet. "You go and shower. You're a mess."

"You're a diamond, Dave, you know that?"

Dave flashes his broad, generous smile as he turns towards the kitchen. "That's right, buddy. You couldn't afford me if you tried."

An hour later I'm standing in Driscoll's bar. The shower, the aspirin, and the inky black coffee that Dave made for me have worked their magic, and I feel human again. I even managed to scrub the wine stains from my lips with my toothbrush, and despite the way they're tingling Dave has reassured me that I don't look like Mick Jagger's love child.

"Buddy, I know it was hard, but it was years ago. And this girl... she's good for you. I haven't seen you this happy in a long time."

Dave is now hard at work trying to convince me to slip my number into Pippa's bag before she leaves, telling me that I'm ready for something more than a snow-lodge fling, when Driscoll's door swings wide open and slams against a nearby table. There, struggling under the weight of a huge backpack and dragging a large duffel bag across the slushy puddle outside the door, is Pippa.

"Hey! Wait up," I call as I bound across the room. Dave's there with me in a second, lifting her bag out of the slush while I ease the backpack from her shoulders. I'd have helped her with her bags anyway, of course, but I'm also relieved to get away from Dave's badgering. He almost had me convinced.

"My knights in shining snow boots!" Pippa grins. She has a dimple, just on the one side, every time she smiles and sometimes when she makes a disappointed frown. It's the most adorable thing.

"I prefer to think of myself as the knight and Aiden as the feckless squire," says Dave, giving me a good dig in the ribs. Pippa laughs and steps into the bar, pulling off her gloves and kicking the snow from her boots on the mat.

"And now, Madame," Dave continues, with exaggerated chivalry, "If you will excuse me, I must away. There's a bus-load of new guests arriving in an hour. Safe journey, Pippa!"

"Aw, that's a shame. It was great meeting you, Dave," Pippa replies warmly, and pulls him in for a hug. They break apart, and Dave gives a little wave as he moves towards the door. As soon as Pippa turns back to face me, Dave gestures wildly to her bags and mouths "Your number!", then gives me a big cheesy grin and two thumbs up.

"Coffee?" I blurt out, trying to move her away from the door while subtly shooing Dave away. She nods, and heads off to find a seat. There's something sad about the smile she gives me before she turns away, and the entire time I'm waiting at the bar, it eats at me.

Dave's sister, Anna, is working the bar. We chit chat about the weather, and by the time she's done pouring two coffees, I've managed to convince myself that Pippa's sadness is caused by the end of her vacation, rather than by the end of her time with me. She's been very clear, several times, about wanting this to be a vacation-only thing, and much as I'd love to slip her my number as Dave suggested, it wouldn't be fair. I promised her I wouldn't push my luck at least half-a-dozen times over that first couple of insane, exhilarating, sex-filled days.

Maybe, once she's gone, I'll just become some sad, lonely loser who let the right girl slip away, bitter because he was too distracted by her dynamite body and her gripping personality to make the right moves. Too wrapped up in an old teenage tragedy to be a man.

I place Pippa's coffee down in front of her and take a seat beside her, sipping on my own drink.

"Were you hungover this morning?" I ask. "I felt like death."

She snorts. "Morning my ass, Aiden. I didn't leave until after noon and you were still passed out. That's what we get for drinking until the wee hours. You're the lucky one though, right? You don't have half a day of traveling ahead of you."

I half-smile and nod, but in my head, I'm immediately trying to figure out if she means a literal half day—and if so, which cities are a twelve-hour trip from here, if you account for the drive to the airport, the security checks, the travel on the other side. As I'm trying to work out whether she's the type to check in two hours early or right at the last second, she waves her hand in front of my face.

"What?" I say, noting her expectant look.

"I asked what you have planned for tonight," she says, her head slightly tilted. "Still a little hungover?"

"A little," I say, nodding and taking another sip of coffee. "I'll probably just find something to watch and stay in. I'm too old for all these late nights, now."

She laughs. "You're twenty-eight," she says. "Get a grip."

We laugh together, and for a while, it breaks through the unspoken tension that's been lingering between us since she walked in. We manage to talk a couple of hours away, sharing opinions about TV shows and movies. She is aghast that I've never watched *Titanic*, and I can't believe she's never seen *The Shawshank Redemption*.

"It's the best movie of all time, for Christ's sake!" I say, exasperated. Our laughter is interrupted by a loud honking from outside. We both turn and look out the window to see a cab sitting there, its engine running. The driver gets out and walks carefully around to open the trunk.

"Well, that's me," says Pippa. She pushes her long-cold cup away from the edge of the table and gets up, and I follow.

My heart sinks. I have to fight harder than I'd like to against the nagging feeling that this is the part in the movie where the guy declares his undying love for the girl and pulls some huge gesture out of nowhere to make her stay. But this isn't a movie, and I'm not that guy. This is real life, and sometimes it just sucks.

"I had a great time," she says. She looks almost awkward.

"Pippa?" the cab driver calls, poking his head through the door. She waves to him.

"Me, too," I say, for want of far more fitting words. A great time doesn't even begin to cover it.

"These yours, darlin'?" the cabbie asks, gesturing to her bags. She nods, and he starts to drag them out to the car.

My heart is beating faster now that the moment is here. She looks uncertain of what to do, so I make the decision for her.

"The time of my life," I tell her, stepping closer. I push a stray strand of hair out of her face and she looks up. Her huge, blue eyes look almost watery, but it's probably just wishful thinking on my part.

I lean down and kiss her, gently at first, pressing my lips to hers and enjoying the softness as I sink into it. I snake my arm around her waist and pull her closer, kiss her deeper. She opens for me just as she has so many times over the last week, and leans into me, as though she trusts me with her very life. It's perfect. A perfect moment to end a perfect week with a perfect girl.

The trunk of the cab slams closed just as we break reluctantly apart.

"Better go," she says, her voice slightly shaky.

I nod, against my better judgment. "Better go," I agree, and give her one last kiss on her forehead.

She takes a deep breath and straightens her shoulders like she's steeling herself, then steps back.

"Right," she says. "Bye, Aiden. Stay awesome."

"Bye, Pip," I say, and like a prime asshole, I stand there and watch her walk out of the door. I have a view of her profile as she smiles at the cab driver and gets in without glancing back. The door of the cab closes, a clump of pure white snow falls from the side mirror into the dirty, slushy puddle below, and the car pulls away. And just like that, she's gone.

Forever.

PIPPA

December 10, 2018

I run my hands one last time down the sides of the sculpture, over what will eventually be the waist of a mermaid. I've been commissioned to make this statue for a children's hospital on the other side of the city. I've taken to working with mixed materials over the last couple of years, and the results are strewn all around me here in my studio, but they wanted this one done entirely in clay. It's nice to get back to basics.

My thumbs drag inward, molding as they go. I release the pressure slowly, making sure I have just the right curve to lead into the huge tail that will be the focus of the piece. At least for anyone who knows anything about sculpture. The kids will love the open, smiling face the most—at least, that's my hope.

"Knock, knock."

The voice makes me jump, but I recognize it almost immediately.

"Val!" I say, delighted. I remove my hands from my work and pick up my cloth to wipe away the clay. "I didn't know you were coming by this evening. Did you get off early?"

It's 5:30 pm, so hardly early, but by Valerie's standards it's practically a half-day.

"Nah," she says, shaking her head. "I was at a meeting just a couple of blocks away, so I figured I'd call in and see my BFF before I head back to the office."

"Ah," I say, a little disappointed that she's not staying. "Good meeting?"

"Yeah," she says. "It's a new client. One that came over with the merger."

"The new big-shot partner?" I ask.

"Equity partner, yeah. He's starting in the office tomorrow. It's a whole load of work. Everything's crazy right now."

"You think he's going to be a taskmaster, then?" I ask, looking at her with concern. She works quite enough already. She's barely ever at home in our shared apartment, other than to sleep.

She shrugs and shakes her head. "Not according to Alex. You remember him from college? He was in my class. I think he came to our Halloween party in senior year."

"The tall guy with the glasses? Red hair?"

"That's him. He's been working for this guy down in Chicago. Apparently, he's pretty chilled out as long as things get done. Relaxed management style but great at what he does. I guess he'd have to be. He's starting on 5 mill a year, before PPP."

"Five million dollars?" I splutter, wide-eyed. "What's PPP?"

"Profits per partner. He gets a share of whatever the company makes. He's only twenty-nine, too."

"Shit, ask him if he needs any sculptures!" I laugh.

Valerie laughs too, and eyes the piece I've been working on. "This is looking great, Pips," she says, nodding to it. "It's

15

the one for the kids' hospital, right? It's really taking shape now."

I move a couple of steps to stand beside her so I have the same vantage point she does. I've been deep into it for a few hours, sculpting the general shapes and curves, and this is the first time I'm getting a proper look at it.

"Yeah, it's not actually that bad," I say, nodding.

"High praise," says Valerie, deadpan. "But it's nice to see you getting into it again."

It's true that I haven't really been able to find my mojo. Not since the ski trip back in March. I came back and wallowed at home for a couple of weeks, triggering an intervention from Valerie. I quit drinking alcohol, got back into the gym, and cleaned up my diet. I'm even meditating every day. I've lost a little weight, even if the last few pounds hanging around my tummy are the most stubborn thing in the world. Despite practically living the *Eat, Pray, Love* lifestyle ever since, I still haven't really found myself able to come up with ideas for original pieces. Thoughts of Aiden have been too invasive and too frequent. I feel a little embarrassed to still be thinking about a week-long vacation fling, all this time later.

I did go on a few dates back in August, after much nagging from Valerie, but they were all complete disasters. Despite my best intentions, I ended up judging every guy against the standard Aiden set, and they all ended up looking like shadows by comparison.

"I'm going to make a lasagne when I get home," I say, feeling a sudden need to change the subject. "I'll leave a plate in the microwave."

"You're the best," says Val, checking the phone that just buzzed in her purse. "And alas, I have to get back." She leans in to kiss me on the cheek, and I give her a quick squeeze.

"See you later."

"Be good," she says, and heads back out, calling "Don't work too late!" without even a hint of irony.

After she's gone, I take one last look at the piece I've been working on and decide that Valerie is right. It's a good place to stop. I'll come back tomorrow and start working on the details. Cutting and applying a gazillion clay scales by hand isn't a job to start on a Monday evening. I wash my hands, tidy up my tools, and lock up the studio.

I usually get a bus home or call a cab, but the air outside is crisp and wintry, and with Christmas only a couple of weeks away I decide to walk, thinking it might help get me into the holiday spirit. Besides, my feet have been swelling a little lately when I stand still for too long in the studio, so I could probably do with getting some more exercise. It'll take an hour, and I'll have to walk by the swanky out-of-town bars and restaurants that all popped up a few years ago when some hipsters from the city decided that this area was "quaint", but I'm sure they'll all be too busy with their own thing to pay much attention to the scruffy, clay-smeared combat pants I have on.

It's rather pleasant, actually. There's a coffee stand just down the street from the studio, so I stop by and get a cup to warm my hands as I walk. Fingerless gloves are great for wearing in the studio when it's cold, but terrible for actually keeping your fingers warm.

The streets are all decorated with twinkling lights, and the pre-Christmas party season is in full swing. Office workers still in their suits spill out of bars and into the street to light up cigarettes, with festive music floating out behind them. I glance through all the windows, noting the differences between the bars. Some are rowdy and full of wait staff in casual gear, and some are much more upmarket, with waiters in dress pants and shirts. In one place, they even wear cummerbunds as part of their uniform.

It's a glance into one of the more expensive-looking

places that stops me dead in my tracks. My brows rise in surprise before my mind has had time to catch up, and I look again. My breath hitches. I blink, hard, and feel cold on my fingertips before I even realize I've touched the window.

Him.

There, sitting at a table across from a woman with beautiful blonde hair swept up into an elegant twist, is Aiden. *My Aiden,* I think, before I can catch myself.

It was a week-long fling, and it was months ago. And I asked him, again and again, to let it be no more than that. And he's gorgeous. Of course he's having dinner with some elegant supermodel-type in some swanky restaurant. Maybe he's been with her since before March. It's not like I asked. And yet, despite knowing how crazy and inappropriate it is, I feel a knot of jealousy tie itself into my gut.

I'm transfixed, watching him chat and sip wine. There's a smoker standing beside me, puffing fumes in my direction. It stinks, and he's staring at me, but I'm too wrapped up in this sudden vision of Aiden to be bothered by it.

The smoke clears from in front of me and I can see him again, laughing, and then the laugh freezes on his face. He's looking right at me, and I can tell in an instant that he's recognized me.

"Shit," I hiss, feeling my throat constrict suddenly. My heart is fluttering in my chest like a captive bird, and I quickly pull back from the window. I'm not over him. Not even a little bit. As much as I've tried to kid myself these last few months, it took only a split second of seeing him for me to realize what a lie that was. And I really don't want him to introduce me to the blonde supermodel as an "old friend", or whatever other cliche he might come up with.

I tuck my chin to my chest, barge past the smoker with a muttered apology, and walk away from the restaurant as quickly as my aching feet will carry me.

AIDEN

"Cheers, Lexi," I say, holding up my wineglass to toast the woman sitting opposite me, for the third time tonight. She looks stunning in her tailored suit, with her hair swept up high on her head. But then, she always looks stunning.

"Cheers," she replies, beaming at me. "I still can't believe you're finally here!"

"I can," I say, with a wry smile. "I wrote my first rent check yesterday, and it sure as hell reminded me that I've arrived in New York."

"It's a lovely place, though. The bed is so comfortable. I could barely drag myself out of it this morning. Do yo—"

She's interrupted by the arrival of the waiter at the table, who's come to bring us the wine Lexi chose from the menu. I should have known one bottle wouldn't be enough for the two of us. The waiter turns the bottle around so the label is facing us, and for a moment I'm thrown off balance. I recognize it from the lodge. It's the very same wine, from the same year, as the bottle I shared with Pippa on that last night in the cabin.

The memory is sudden and evocative. I can smell the

burning fire, hear the sound of her laugh, taste the slight saltiness of the skin just below her navel.

"AIDEN!"

Lexi's voice startles me out of my daydream and I look over to her. "Huh?"

"I asked if you wanted to try it."

"Oh," I say, looking up at the waiter with a short shake of my head. "No, thanks. Go ahead."

"Do you think you'll buy somewhere in the city?" Lexi asks as the waiter pours into two fresh glasses.

"Mmm," I say, still half distracted. I force myself out of my memories, determined to give Lexi my full attention. She is here and Pippa is not, and I have no desire to be rude. "Maybe. Depends how the new job goes. I've taken a big risk."

"For a big reward," Lexi interjects.

She's always been an ambitious go-getter. You don't co-found one of the most successful women's magazines in the country by being a content little wallflower. Lexi always looks amazing, always has designer this or on-trend that, but it's mostly because she has to keep up appearances for her job. Deep down, she's a sweetheart.

"How's work?" I ask, changing the subject, and she's off.

All the way through the appetizer and halfway through the entrée, she regales me with tales about her magazine, the shenanigans of the staff and the latest celebrity gossip. I gasp and laugh in all the right places, as I gradually forget about Pippa and start to enjoy being in the moment with Lexi again. She tells me one story about a famous power couple who ended up having the cops called on them when they had a huge fight in front of their very large mansion on their very upmarket Beverly Hills street, and—just as I'm thinking she won't be able to top that—another one about a well-known actor who ended up in the ER with a deodorant canister stuck up his rear.

I'm still laughing when my eye happens to catch a face looking through the window. For a moment, as my mind tries to make sense of what it's seeing, time seems to stand still. I can feel the smile fall from my lips as a shock wave washes over me. It can't be her. It can't be. The odds of her actually being at that window are so astronomical that it's seriously more likely that I've just gone mad. I blink, half-expecting her face to vanish in that instant, but when I open my eyes, she's still there. Those beautiful blue eyes are wide and locked with mine, and every sinew of my body is suddenly coiled like a spring.

"Aiden?" Lexi says, but her voice comes to me like it's traveling through a thick fog.

I blink again and Pippa is gone, but I see the tail end of her scarf as it disappears from view. Without another thought, I jump to my feet. I hear the clonk of a wine glass toppling, and Lexi gasps.

"No," I say, low and determined. There's a shattering sound and a murmuring around us. A fussing waiter appears, dabbing at my wine-covered pants. My blood is running hot and my mind is filled with nothing but the desire to catch her. This must be how a predator feels when their prey spots them and bolts. And now she has a head start.

"Not again," I hear myself growl. I shove past the waiter and stalk across the restaurant, past the staring diners and out into the bitterly cold night.

PIPPA

"**E**xcuse me," I hiss as I round the corner, trying to squeeze myself through the crowd.

I don't know where I'm going, but I know I have to go. My heart is hammering after seeing him, but the sight of the beautiful woman sitting opposite him, looking so natural and so comfortable with him, has left a deep sinking feeling in the pit of my stomach.

Better not to have seen him. Better if I scrub this from my memory and pretend it never happened.

"Hey, watch it!" says a woman in a stunning black dress as I pass. I shoot her an apologetic smile, but she looks me up and down, notes the clay stains all over my baggy pants, and gives me a withering look.

"Here," says a man as I turn around. I look up at him, note the expression of pity on his face, and before I can say anything he's dropped a few coins into my coffee cup.

Mortifying. But there's no time to stop and tell him I'm an artist—not a homeless person—because even this won't be as mortifying as if Aiden catches me. Even as I press on, squeezing here and ducking there, drawing scornful protests and contemptuous looks from those I barrel past, I'm angry at myself for even thinking that he would leave the cozy little restaurant with that stunning blonde to come after me.

Who was she? Girlfriend? Wife? The thought of it makes me feel like a cold hand has wrapped itself around my throat and started squeezing. Was he married that whole time at the lodge?

"PIPPA!"

It's distant, but it's him. Unmistakably him. My heart jumps into my throat and I stop dead in my tracks. This is fight or flight. Every ounce of my brain is telling me to move forward. Every piece of my heart is telling me to turn around and find him. I'm vaguely aware of the coffee cup slipping from my hand as I stand there, frozen to the spot.

Tick, tock.

Seconds roll by, but they feel like hours. The cup hits the floor in slow motion. A coin jumps out and rolls away, coming to rest between two cobblestones. Still-warm coffee splashes everywhere, spattering thick, dark droplets across the tailored pants and bare legs of the street revelers all around me.

"PIPPA!"

Closer now.

His voice finally spurs me to action, and flight wins out. I dive into the crowd ahead of me, gripping my backpack tighter, ducking and weaving as best I can to get away.

"Sorry," I say, every few steps. "Coming through. Sorry!"

The end of the street is in sight, now. I can turn left, and if the road is less crowded than this one, I can be in the next back-alley in seconds. There has to be a dumpster or something I can hide behind.

There's a gaggle of people outside one of the bars, taking a photo, and even in my current state I'm polite enough to stop and wait for them to take their picture. How much difference will a few seconds make?

"Pip."

23

A lot of difference.

I'm frozen again. His voice came from right behind me. I could turn right now and look at his beautiful face, but how can I? What will I say? Every inch of my body is tingling with adrenaline, and there's a lump rising in my throat. In all my twenty-four years, I've never been so thrilled and so scared at once.

"Pippa."

There's an edge to his voice this time, an insistence, and I know that he won't take no for an answer. My eyes close, and I squeeze them hard before opening them and taking a deep breath. And then, of all the things I could say and all the things I could do—from slapping him across the face to falling into his arms—I choose the worst possible option.

AIDEN

"**W**here did she go?" I demand of the man outside, who blows a thick plume of smoke and steam out of the side of his mouth. I must look frantic, swiveling my head around as I try to find her.

He stares at me, blankly.

"The girl!" My voice is louder and more insistent than strictly necessary. "She was here just a minute ago. Blue eyes, dark hair, pretty. About this tall," I say, holding a hand up at the middle of my chest.

His eyes look glassy, like he's had a couple too many at his office Christmas party, and I briefly consider strangling him. Finally, as my question seeps into his brain, he lifts his cigarette and jabs it toward the narrow street that runs down along the side of the restaurant.

Muttering my thanks, I take off after her. Long strides carrying me around the corner, but I have to skid to a stop almost immediately. It really is busy in this part of town tonight. There are Christmas bauble earrings and Santa hats on almost everyone I look at, and lights flash between fir branches in every window, making the narrow alley light up like one big dance floor.

"Pippa!" I call, but the voices of the revelers and the music piping out of the bars drown me out.

I move a bit faster, shoving people out of the way left and right, my eyes frantically scanning the crowd for her. A glance behind me and I'm already halfway down the street. If I reach the end without finding her, I'm only going to have a fifty-fifty chance of turning the right way.

"PIPPA!" I shout louder, desperate now. My voice carries and my pace is such that people have started to make way in front of me, parting like a booze-soaked Red Sea.

They all move, left and right, clearing a path down the middle of the alley and allowing me to pick up my pace until I'm running, closer and closer toward the end of the street, where I might lose her forever for the second time. The cold air is burning my throat and lungs with every breath, and my head is spinning from the wine and the running.

Just as I can feel myself beginning to lose hope, right at the very end of the street, the crowd parts and the way is suddenly clear. Clear of everything but one small figure in a thick coat, carrying a heavy backpack, and... muddy combat pants?

"Pip?" I say, barely a few feet behind her. She's stopped dead.

"Pippa," I say again, between heavy breaths. I hear my own voice and there's something a little harsh in it this time, something that demands she face me now that I've caught her fair and square. She turns around, slowly. I don't know what I'm expecting her to say or do... but I certainly don't expect what happens next.

With feigned surprise, she glances to me and then looks off to the side, not meeting my eye. "Oh hey, Aiden," she says nonchalantly, as though she hadn't even seen me back at the restaurant. I stare at her in disbelief. Is she... trying to be casual? I might buy it, if it weren't for that little quaver in her voice.

After all the adrenaline, the way she's trying to act like an ice princess while I'm standing here feeling everything at once, infuriates me.

"Are you trying to act cool?" I demand, sounding a bit like an asshole.

I regret it immediately. I've never been so happy, just seconds after never having been so terrified, and it's messing with my composure. She looks down toward my feet, then up to my face again. I search her features for emotion, and I'm horrified to see tears glittering along her lower lids. Her bottom lip trembles, and she blurts out, half sobbing: "Your pants!"

"What?" I ask, confused. I follow her gaze down. The pale gray material is covered in dark blotches of wine, but that can't be why she's crying, right?

"Oh God. Jesus. Shit," she's saying, dabbing furiously at her eyes with the sleeve of her coat. She looks ridiculous. And adorable. "I'm crying!" she exclaims.

The sudden urge to reach out and pull her into a hug is overwhelming, but given her reaction to seeing me again, running off and then... whatever this is—I'm not sure it'd be welcome. There's a group of people just ahead of her who look like they've been taking photos, and they're starting to pay more and more attention to us.

"You have no room to talk about pants, little Pip," I say, moving a little closer. Thankfully, I've got my voice back under control. I sound as happy to see her as I feel, and nothing like the dick who spoke a moment ago.

She looks down at her own pants, then up at me. I smile at her, and her face just breaks open with laughter. She's tearful and snotty and captivating, and still going to town with her sleeve, dabbing at her watery eyes.

"Stop," I say quietly, gently taking her arm and pulling it away from her face. I want to see her—and I'm afraid she might rub her perfect little nose away if she keeps this up.

She looks at me again, her huge blue eyes framed with dark lashes that glisten with captured tears. I reach up and push a stray hair out of her face, and she drops her head, almost bashful.

"Oh, God. I'm such a mess," she says.

"You're beautiful," I tell her, crooking a finger under her chin and lifting her head so I can see her.

"What the hell are you doing here?" she asks, her voice a strained whisper.

"I just moved here." I watch her head snap sharply upward, as though she's looking for the lie in my face. "What the hell are you doing here?" I ask. I suspect the answer already, and I can hear the smile in my voice.

"I… I live here, too," Pippa says, with a watery smile.

So I kiss her. And the onlookers cheer.

PIPPA

I can scarcely believe it when he says he just moved here.
Something inside me lifts and I return the smile he's
giving me, almost forgetting how much of an absolute
mess I look. Scruffy, clay-covered pants, a coat that makes
me look like the Michelin man, fingerless gloves, a huge
backpack—oh, and a puffy, red, teary face, just to top off the
look.

"I... I live here, too."

I stammer out my reply to him, and suddenly I am warm
and safe, floating on air. His lips are on mine, and it's as
though not a second has passed since that wonderful week in
March. His tongue probes my mouth, his finger and thumb
keep their grip on my chin a moment, before his hand goes
to my shoulder and slips the heavy pack off it, as though it
were light as a feather.

He tastes of wine and smells of masculine, musky after-
shave. I place my hands on his shoulders as though it were
the most natural thing in the world, and he rests a hand
gently on my jawline, probing my mouth with his tongue.

I surrender to him, just the way I did that first night in

the resort, my body leaning into him as my mind floats elsewhere, on another plane, brimming with happiness. I'm peripherally aware of the cheering crowd around us, but I can't bring myself to feel self-conscious. He is beautiful, and this, this kiss, the way he holds me, the way he gently coaxes me to respond and let my tongue dance with his, feels so good I never want to be anywhere else. Not in all the many nights I fantasized about this moment did I ever expect it to be this perfect. This... right.

"AIDEN!"

He groans into my mouth and pulls his head back. I feel instantly exposed, and briefly flash an embarrassed smile to the people who are still clapping. And then, I see her.

Her.

From the restaurant. Standing there in a tailored coat, looking stunning, holding another coat—a man's coat. Aiden's coat? As she walks around to his side, she notices me and looks me quickly up and down. Her gaze moves around, taking in the scene. Aiden's hand still on my jaw, the flushed pink of my lips, my arms around his shoulders. And she looks... amused.

"Lexi," says Aiden, finally removing his hand from my jaw and leaving me feeling bereft as the cold night air moves in to take its place. I'm slightly reassured when he slides his hand down and pushes his fingers between mine, turning so that he's standing by my side, facing her. I'm not sure I'm ready for whatever showdown is about to happen, though.

"You forgot your coat, darling," says the blonde, holding it out to him on one perfectly manicured finger. Amusement sparkles in her eyes. He takes the coat with his free hand.

The second she calls him "darling," I tense. He must sense it, because he squeezes my hand reassuringly.

"Thanks. Hey, Lexi, meet Pippa," he says, looking to me. I glance up from where I've been admiring her killer kitten heels and smile timidly. I'm surprised to see her big, brown Bambi eyes go wide as she stares at me.

"Pippa?" she splutters, looking from me to Aiden and back again. She glances down at my pants again, but there's very little I can do now to stop myself standing out like a sore thumb.

"Pippa Pippa?" she asks Aiden, still looking shocked. "From the resort?"

He gives a quick nod, grinning.

"Oh my God!" she says. She looks… delighted. "I don't believe it!"

"Me either," says Aiden.

"Me either," I say, and the two of them laugh. I still have no clue who she is, so I'm a bit guarded as this intimidatingly beautiful woman stands there looking at me like I'm some sort of long-lost friend. I start to wonder if I'm the butt of some joke in an open relationship. But then again, I do have a habit of letting my imagination run wild—so I push the thought to the back of my mind and just stand there, waiting for someone to explain what the hell is going on.

"Pippa," says Aiden. "This is my sister, Lexi. She's staying in my apartment for a couple of days to help me get settled in."

The relief that washes over me is palpable. I swear my shoulders sag a couple of inches as my body unties itself from the knot of tension it had twisted into, and my lips melt from a forced grin to a genuine smile.

"Oh. Oh! Hey!" I manage, not really knowing what else to say—and not knowing why her reaction to me being "Pippa Pippa" was so enthusiastic. That has to be a good thing, right?

She looks from Aiden to me again, and then takes a step back, as though she suddenly feels like an intruder.

"Well I need to settle the check," she says, still beaming. "It

31

was great to meet you, Pippa. I hope we meet again." She looks to Aiden. "Get her number this time, idiot."

Aiden shoos her away, but she's already heading down the street, taking the cobblestone with ease even in her three-inch heels, and the crowds are parting for her as she goes.

"She does make a good point," says Aiden, turning back to me.

"Mhmm," I grin. I've finally found a little equilibrium in the chaos. "But we have a tradition," I say, and he lets out a half-laughing groan.

I had forgotten how gorgeous he was until I saw him again. He'd faded with time in my memory, but now that he's here I can't bear to look away from him.

"Tell you what," I say, ducking down to my backpack. I take out a notepad and pen and start writing out my studio's address. "I have to get home right now, because I've promised my roommate I'll make a lasagne, and she's been working crazy hours.

"Oh, Vicky, right? Something with a V?" he asks, looking amused.

"Something like that," I say, recalling the moment in the cabin when I accidentally let slip that little snippet about life back home, and then demanded he forget it immediately. I finish scribbling the note and hand it to him.

"This is where I work. I'm there every day until at least five. Come by and see me."

"You're not giving me your number?" he asks, incredulous, as he scans the note and pockets it.

"Where's the fun in that?" I ask. "And besides. I feel like you have to work for it now, after making me think you were dating some stunning blonde."

Aiden looks puzzled for a moment, and then realization dawns on his face. "Oh! You thought..." he looks over his shoulder in the direction that Lexi disappeared. "Wow.

Okay." He looks back down at me, and he's smirking a little. I can tell that my disappearing act and terrible attempt at an ice queen routine suddenly make a lot more sense to him.

"I can hardly be held accountable for your overactive imagination," he says.

"Yes you can," I correct him. "And you are. And besides, it's more fun this way."

"Pippa," he says, seriously. All humor has gone from him as he takes my hand. I feel my heart beating hard inside my chest, and the casual air I've been trying to hold is faltering on my face. "Swear to me this is the right address, or so help me I will kidnap you from this very spot and chain you up in my new apartment. I can't lose you again."

He speaks so candidly and mirrors my own fears back at me in such high definition that it's hard to keep looking at him. I want to jump in a cab with him and disappear into the sunset so badly that his offer of kidnap is almost tempting. But I have to take things slowly this time and not jump in head first. Living in the same city - maybe even the same neighborhood - is a very different deal than a week-long vacation fling.

I push up to the very tips of my toes and place my hand on the side of his face. He indulges me, leaning down, and I press a soft kiss to his lips

"I swear."

"Fine," he sighs, stealing a last kiss. "Can I get you a cab? Walk you somewhere?"

I shake my head, grinning stupidly. No. I want to savor this, and the walk home will let me mull over every precious detail. "Thanks, but I'm good. I'll see you tomorrow. Or whenever. Right?" Grabbing my backpack, I heave it up over my shoulder.

"Not tomorrow," he says, looking apologetic. "Sorry, Pip. First day at my new office. Wednesday? Dinner?" he asks.

"Pick you up at this place," he pats the pocket where he stashed the note. "Say, eight?"

"It's a date!"

I turn around and start walking, somehow resisting the urge to look back. Swollen as they are, I have to trust my feet to carry me home—because my head is already in the clouds.

AIDEN

December 12, 2018

Yesterday, my first day in the office, did not go well. Not as well as I'd hoped it would, at least. I'm the newest equity partner, the existing partners having taken a chance on me based on the reputation and client base I managed to build up in Chicago, and these next few months are going to be crucial for me in making sure they don't regret that decision. How the hell I'm going to pull that off is anyone's guess, if yesterday is anything to go by.

Thank God for Valerie. She's the associate whose job it is to bring me up to speed and merge my clients into the firm, and she's smart as a whip. She'll make partner in no time. She probably thinks I'm a moron, given how many times she's caught me daydreaming in my office, staring out of the window. Pippa has been on my mind ever since I saw her face in the restaurant window on Monday evening, and I can barely think of anything else. I can't wait to see her tonight.

Today, Wednesday, I've decided to be more proactive.

Stepping out of my huge, open corner office, I stride down a short corridor and into the room that Valerie shares with another couple of associates. The door is open, and she's on the phone with her back to me.

"How about that little black dress with the lace trim?" she says into her phone. "You can borrow my Louboutins if you like. They're in my closet. Top shelf." One of the other associates has looked up from her desk and noticed me standing in the doorway, and I can see her looking to Valerie, trying to tell her with wide eyes that the new boss just walked in.

Valerie doesn't notice. There's a pause, presumably as whoever is on the other end of the line responds, and then she speaks again. "Well you have a few hours. Just practice a bit in front of the mirror." Another pause, and she sighs. "Alright, well there's some Viviers there that are not too high. Just have a look and see what's comfortable. Borrow whatever you like. But I want you to know you'd have looked killer in the Loubou—"

She cuts off, apparently having noticed the increasingly urgent bug eyes from her colleague, and snaps her head around. Her eyes widen slightly when she sees me standing behind her.

"Oh. Gotta go," she says into her phone. "See you later."

Thumbing away the call, she places her phone down on her desk, stands up, and smiles, straightening her pencil skirt. "Hey," she says, searching my face. "Everything alright?"

"Yeah," I nod. "All good. I wondered if you had time to come and look over the Mackenzie file with me. It's due for litigation early in January and I want to get a jump on it."

"Oh, sure," she says, grabbing her phone again. She unplugs her laptop and flips it shut, tucking it under her arm to follow me back to my office.

We spend the rest of the afternoon going over the file, debating the merits of one approach after another, bouncing ideas back and forth until finally, when it's been dark outside for a couple of hours already, we hit upon a strategy that we both think is airtight. My mind wanders now and then to Pippa, and there's a constant hum of excitement running through me at the prospect of taking her to dinner tonight, but at least it seems that I've managed to impress Valerie today.

"Oh, shit," I say, looking at the clock as it ticks over to 7:34 pm. "I have to get going. Meeting someone for dinner." I stand up and grab my jacket, shrugging it on and collecting my other belongings. I push the button on the intercom.

"Dominic," I say to my secretary. "Can you have a car ready ASAP, please?"

"I'll call down now, Sir," he replies over the intercom, his voice tinny through the speaker. "It should be ready by the time you reach the lobby."

"Thanks," I say, releasing the button. I pat down my pockets to be sure I have everything.

"Can you get this rolling?" I ask Valerie. "Have Dominic send the final notice letter tomorrow and we'll take it from there."

"Of course, Mr. Coleman," she says, professionally, and she's on her feet in seconds, laptop under her arm again, ready to set to work.

"Aiden is fine."

"Of course, Aiden," she says, with a little nod of her head. "Have a good evening." She smiles and strides out of my office.

I arrive outside the address written on the scrap of paper at exactly 7:58 pm and quickly send the driver away. Pippa knows nothing about me or my life, and in some ways I think that's what made the week at the lodge so magical. She'll inevitably find out at some point—I hope—but there's no need to show off with chauffeur-driven cars and fancy restaurants. I have a sneaking suspicion she'd find it off-putting, which is part of what I like about her.

The building in front of me is a little box of bricks with a single, metal door. There's no signage or hint as to what's inside, and the way the surrounding area is built up into commercial structures full of chain stores gives me the distinct impression that the little brick box is the property of a very stubborn owner indeed.

Just to be sure, I pull up a map on my phone and cross-reference it with the note in my hand. Sure enough, this seems to be the place. Shoving my things back in my pockets, I step up to the door and bang on it with the side of my fist a few times.

The excitement that's been brewing all day is bubbling to the surface now. I can't wait to see her, and I'm very curious to see what she does for a living. Based on what she was wearing the other day when she said she was just off work, I'd half expected to pull up to a building site to see her laying bricks.

I can hear some clanging and clunking inside that sounds like bolts and locks being undone, and the heavy door swings open.

I gape.

Pippa is standing there in the doorway with her hair swept up into a half-messy top knot, wearing a long-sleeved black dress that hugs her waist and falls down to a mid-thigh strip of lace. She's wearing makeup, but only just enough to accentuate her already-stunning features, and black, knee-high boots with a small heel that makes her a little taller. Her legs are dark with sheer black tights. Or maybe stockings. I don't know which, but now that I've noticed them I have a sudden, desperate urge to find out. She looks a little nervous as I stand there appraising her.

"Wow," I say, finally finding my voice. "You look amazing."

Her face breaks into a smile and she stands aside to let me in.

"Thanks," she says. "You don't look so bad yourself. Come in, I just have to get a couple of things and finish up, then we can go. Mind the doo—"

She says it just as I walk forward and hit the top of my forehead on the inner door frame. "Shit!" I exclaim, rubbing at the spot.

"Sorry!" she says, pointing up at it. She's half giggling. "I should have warned you earlier. Are you alright?"

I'm fine. The amused sparkle in her eyes and the laugh in her voice is tonic enough for the pain. Not to mention the sight of her swaying ass as she walks ahead of me.

"I'm good," I reply, as I gradually pull my eyes away from her to look at the room I've just stepped into.

The space inside is entirely open plan. There are sculptures all around, some half-finished, some complete. There are complex metal compositions and simpler clay pieces, there are workbenches full of tools and materials, and in the middle of the room, sitting on a small, wooden platform, is what I assume to be the current work in progress. There's not much detail yet, but the shape is unmistakably a mermaid.

"You're a sculptor," I say, taking it all in.

She nods, a smile on her face, watching my reaction.

I had no clue what she did before I set foot in here, but now it makes total sense. I can almost feel her personality oozing from the finished pieces.

"Wow, there's some really stunning stuff here, Pip," I say, running my fingers down the length of a metal bar beside me. It's part of a mother and child piece. Metal balls sit as the heads of the characters, while thick wire and metal plates twist around each other and form the limbs. The pose of the mother, bent over her child with her arms swept protectively around him, is so evocative I feel my breath catch. I don't know much about art, but I know it must take real skill to draw out that kind of emotional reaction just by twining pieces of metal together.

I look up and she's watching me, her head slightly tilted.

"I couldn't bring myself to sell that one," she says, smiling.

"I love it," I tell her, straightening up again.

A silence hangs in the air for a moment, before she claps her hands together.

"Right! Won't be a moment," she says, and in her lovely little dress, she sashays across the room and bends over a workbench, careful not to get any dust or clay on herself. I hear the clinking of tools as she finishes packing up.

The sight of her from behind almost undoes me. Her legs are shapely and long, and the curve of her hip is accentuated by the way she's bent slightly forward. She reaches for something right at the back of the bench, and the dress rides up a little.

Stockings. The lace at the top of them matches the lace at the bottom of her dress, and there's a thin line of supple flesh in between. I feel my balls clench upward and a twitch in my pants. Without even thinking about it, I'm right behind her in three long strides, my hands on her hips and my lips on the side of her neck. She smells of a feminine perfume with a hint of cherry and a dash of white musk. It's the same perfume she was wearing in the cabin, and my mind swirls with those same emotions.

She has stopped tidying away her tools, but she doesn't turn around.

Greedy lust has overtaken me, and I pull her hips back and press myself against her rear, so she can feel me, fully hard, straining against my pants.

"We'll be late," she whispers, but at the same time, she pushes her hips back against me, tilting her ass upward.

My hands are on my belt, almost fumbling in the rush to

40

undo it. I slide leather through metal and undo my button and fly.

"I don't care," I tell her, placing my hand in the centre of her back and guiding her forward. She complies just as I let my pants and underwear fall halfway down my thighs and take my cock in my hand. I stroke it slowly as I peel the dress up over her ass and take a moment to admire the expanse of pale flesh against the dark stockings, dress and thong she's wearing. "I have to have you now."

I hook my finger in behind the string of the thong and slide it down, pulling it to the side. The anticipation is killing me. My skin is tingling all over.

"You'd rather be on time?" I ask her, hearing the breathless edge to my voice as I slide my thumb between her lips and feel her, wet and wanting.

"No." Her voice is slightly strangled with lust, and when I slide my thumb out and trail it down to her clitoris, she lets out a heavy moan.

I am inside her in a second, as deep as I can get, feeling an urge to lose myself in her. In that split second, I remember. I remember the feeling of her body, the taste of her skin, the way she has a habit of giggling just after she comes. It all comes flooding back, and for a moment I fear I'll blow my load instantly, without getting a chance to savor it.

I feel her clenching around me, this beautiful, funny, talented nymph, and I feel like this, right here, is where I could die happy. I start to roll my hips, slowly, teasing quiet moans from her. I watch as her arms stretch out across the bench and her fingers hook over the edge of it, gripping gently to steady herself.

I reach around her to find that sensitive little nub of nerve endings with my fingers and start to run circles around it while I fuck her.

"Aiden," she gasps, lifting her ass a little higher. The sight of her makes me groan with lust. I need her. I need to be with her, inside of her. I roll my hips faster and harder, until the sound of my balls slapping against her sex starts to echo from the walls. I reach forward with my free hand, running it down her arm until she releases the end of the bench and I can slot my fingers in between hers. She grips my hand hard, and starts to gasp. I can tell she's pushing closer and closer to her precipice, and I step up my pace.

"Come for me, little Pip," I whisper in her ear, desperate to feel her core clench and twitch around my length.

She sucks in a huge breath and holds it, and I know it's coming. I lean to the side to watch her, to see the little changes in her face. The breath is released as a loud, sighing moan as I feel waves of pressure squeeze at me, driving me toward my own undoing. Her mouth is open, her brows drawn down. There's a flush on her cheeks and her chest. She's never been so beautiful. She shudders and bucks underneath me, and I can hold on no longer.

With a loud grunt, I feel my balls tighten, and I hold deep inside her clenching sheath and empty into her. Finally, at last, all the many long months of missing her, of wanting her, are over.

She's still twitching when the adorable giggle bubbles from her mouth, and I chase it down, swallow it as I press my mouth to hers, pulling her up and around so I can kiss her.

"I uh," she says, between heavy breaths. "Guess I should go clean up."

She looks up at me and bites her lip, smiling, and at that moment I know that we're going to be very, very late to dinner.

PIPPA

By the time we reach the restaurant, our reservation is long gone and every table looks packed. No matter how many yarns Aiden spins about meetings and emergencies, the maitre d' remains impassive. Despite the fact that I spent a full fifteen minutes straightening myself out after the... *activities* back at the studio, and that I've done nothing but sit in a warm taxi since, basking in the afterglow and enjoying the feeling of Aiden's fingers dancing over the back of my hand, I'm still paranoid. I imagine for a moment that the maitre d' is giving me side-eye and judging me, and it makes me reach up and double-check my hair. There's a messy bun, and then there's a plain mess. But it feels alright.

Aiden eventually gives up and leads me out into the street. "Well, I gotta eat after all that exercise," he grins, pulling me into him and leaning down to kiss the top of my head. I could swear he gives it a sniff, too. "Oh, there," he says, nodding. He releases me so I can turn around, and sure enough, there's a place all lit up with a couple of empty tables available just beyond the windows.

"Fancy slumming it?" he asks. The place is nowhere near

as fancy as the one he'd booked. It's a BBQ joint that obviously prides itself on its down-to-earth atmosphere. I'm a little overdressed, but now that he's suggested it, all I can smell are tender ribs and burnt ends. And he's not wrong about having worked up an appetite.

"Perfect," I say, smiling up to him. He leans down and steals another kiss from my lips, and we head across the street. It's so strange that he's here, that we're strolling hand in hand through the city that we now both live in. I can feel myself beginning to hope for a future, and I'm not quite sure how to put the brakes on—or if I really want to anymore.

It's warm inside the BBQ place, cozy and full of chatter. A girl around my age comes over with a huge grin and asks if she can take our coats. A few minutes later we're sat in a small booth with a drink each, and we've ordered a sharing platter that the server has promised will be divine.

"So your sister doesn't live in the city?" I ask.

He gives me a questioning look.

"You said she's staying with you to help you get set up."

"Oh," he nods, and takes a swig of his beer. "Yeah. She lives here, but on the opposite side of town. She works in the city so it was easier for her to stay in my spare room instead of traveling over and back every day. And besides, she's been here in New York for a few years while I've been working in Chicago. It's nice to see my big sister for a while, you know?"

"Yeah," I agree. "What does she do?" I ask, recalling the stunning tailored suit she was wearing, the way she held herself.

"Magazines," he says. "She owns Wirl."

I stare at him for a moment, my brows raised. Wirl—presumably a mashup of woman and girl—is a huge online magazine aimed at women in their twenties. Valerie browses it all the time. "Really? Wow. That's... some achievement. She can't be a day over... what?"

"Thirty," he says, grinning. "She's thirty."

"Isn't that like, the biggest online magazine for young women now?"

"Yeah," he says, nodding. "They just overtook their biggest competitor last month. Lexi was over the moon. She deserves it, though. I've never seen anyone work harder."

I smile at him. He seems genuinely proud of her. "And you?" I ask. "What do you do?"

"Me?" he asks, grinning again. He relaxes back in his chair, and holds his hands out at his sides, making a come hither motion with his fingers as though he's issuing a challenge. "Go on," he says. "Guess."

I narrow my eyes at him, tilting my head. "Hmmm," I say, twisting my mouth and pursing my lips to look more thoughtful. "Well you're wearing a suit, so some sort of office," I say. "Unless you're a plumber who's more fashion-conscious than practical..."

He grins and rolls his eyes at me.

"Or a catalog model who's having a particularly busy workwear season?"

He grabs the napkin from the table in front of him and tosses it over at me. It hits me square in my face and I laugh, picking it up from my lap to throw it back. He catches it.

"Alright, alright," I say. "I don't know. Software engineer?"

He stares at me.

"What?" I ask.

"Babe," he says, and I feel a little ripple of pleasure up my spine at the pet name. "Software engineers are about as likely to wear suits as plumbers."

"Really?"

"Really."

"Oh, well. I don't know. And it's not fair that I don't know, because you know what I do!" I remind him.

"Alright, fine. But it'll cost you," he tells me, and I can see a twitch of a smirk threatening on his lips.

"Cost me what?" I ask, imagining all sorts of filthy things

he might request. The memory of the early evening comes back to me and I can feel my cheeks grow a little hotter.

"Your number," he says. The smile has grown fully onto his mouth now, and he waggles his brows at me. I almost melt on the spot. I want to scrawl my number onto the middle of his bare chest, if I'm honest, but I also sort of like this little game we have going. And despite the absolute whirlwind of that week back in March, him not having my number or any other way of contacting me makes me feel a bit more like we're taking things slowly. Not rushing into anything. If I could spend all day thumbing out messages to this Adonis-like man instead of finishing my mermaid by deadline, I almost certainly would. And that would be no good for anyone.

"One digit," I say, giving him a steely stare.

His smile freezes for a minute, and then he laughs. "Five."

"Two," I say.

"Four," he says, and I feel his foot gently press against my ankle. He sweeps it to the side, opening my legs under the table. A rush of cool air assaults the insides of my thighs, where they're covered by neither stocking nor underwear, and I can feel myself flushing again, craving him. "And lunch on Friday."

"Three," I say, hearing a husky edge to my own voice. "And lunch on Friday. Final offer."

He looks about ready to jump over the table and strip me down again, and were it not for the crowd of onlookers we might attract, I can't say I'd object. I feel so at ease in his company, it's hard to stop myself from letting the barriers I've built up fall away. Just as the sexual tension is getting unbearable, along comes our happy, chatty server to break it.

"One Meat Feast, six way combo for two with the fries and salad bowl," she says, swooping a huge tray down onto the table. "Enjoy!"

"Deal," says Aiden, once we're alone again. "Three digits and lunch on Friday."

I straighten in my seat, start assessing the mountain of food in front of us, and say, as nonchalantly as I can: "Nine. One. Seven."

Aiden has his phone out in a flash, and he's thumbing away at the screen, presumably to save the numbers I've given him. It only takes him a moment, and with a satisfied look on his face he pockets the phone again and looks up at me. "I'm a lawyer."

"Oh!" I say. "So is my roomie. I'd say you should come over and meet her, but she's hardly ever away from the office."

"She's an associate, then?" he asks, and the dread I feel at the prospect of him working the same insane hours as Valerie eases up a little.

"Yeah. I take it it gets better?"

"If you want it to," he says. "But there are plenty of partners practically living in their offices, too. Which firm is she with?"

I freeze, my brow furrowing. "Oh, God," I say, grimacing. "Is it terrible that I can't remember the name of my best friend's company?"

Much to my relief, Aiden laughs, shaking his head. "Not at all." Then, a question seems to occur to him. "Oh, hey," he says.

I look up, expectant.

"Tell me about the building."

"What building?" I ask.

"Your studio. It's right in the middle of a bunch of commercial buildings. So who's the holdout?" He's smiling, looking at me with an amused quirk on his lips, like he's almost certain it's me. I'm flattered.

"Not me," I say. "I could never afford a piece of prime real estate in the middle of New York City. And if I could I'd probably sell it and use the money to buy a nice place further out, with more space."

He tilts his head at me. "You don't like the city?" he asks.

"I like it enough," I say. "My life is here, but I'm not going to charge top dollar for sculptures that are meant for children's hospitals and community centers, so I'll never be really financially comfortable. And I do get more inspiration when I'm closer to nature. Is that terribly cliché?"

"No," he says, shaking his head. He looks thoughtful, like there's something else going on in his head, even though he's listening to my every word.

"But anyway, the building belongs to a man called Mr. Ling. He was a friend of my grandmother, and she rented this place from him way back in the day. She was a seamstress. When Mr. Ling's wife left him, she helped him out a lot, bringing meals for him and his kids, mending their clothes. Of course, he was back on his feet soon enough and he remarried, but he never forgot her kindness. He kept her rent the same and refused to sell even when the development companies were offering him astronomical prices for the place. When my grandmother got old enough to retire, I was just starting to get more serious about sculpture. My parents were sick of me filling up the garage with all sorts of junk, so my grandmother had a word with Mr. Ling and he agreed to rent this place to me."

"For the same price?" he asks.

"Yep. And when she passed a few years ago—"

"Sorry," says Aiden, and he means it.

"Thank you. But yeah, he said I could stay here and he wouldn't raise the rent. So that's what I do. Otherwise I'd be sculpting in the street somewhere, because I sure as hell couldn't afford a studio like that at market price."

"Well then," says Aiden, lifting his beer. "Here's to Mr. Ling."

I smile and lift my sparkling water in return, and Aiden

nods to the food, laying his napkin down across his lap. "Right. Let's dig in. This all looks great."

And it is. There are juicy ribs covered in sticky sauce, fat, char-grilled sausages, blackened little burnt ends that taste like summer, and spicy wings that leave my lips tingling. The side salad is crunchy and delicious, the fries are perfectly cooked, and the whole thing has us licking our fingers and wiping our chins the entire time. The way we chat, it feels like we're a couple. A real couple. There's never an awkward silence or a failed joke. We talk about his apartment and the help Lexi has given him with furnishing it, about the coincidence of us meeting like that in a city of over 8 million, and we reminisce about our vacation in the ski lodge.

"And I still can't ski," I laugh, sitting back, finally, my stomach satisfied by the feast.

"I'll teach you next time," he winks. "If I'm not too rusty. Dave seems to think I'll barely be able to keep my balance on the slopes next season."

"Ahhh," I say, remembering Dave, and trying to ignore the fact that Aiden just said there would be a "next time" at the lodge. My heart is suddenly beating at double pace. "How is he?"

"Great," says Aiden, nodding. "He's coming to stay for Christmas, so you'll get to see him, I hope."

My heart does a little leap. Not because of Dave, though from our short acquaintance he seems like a great guy—but because Aiden is talking as though we'll be spending time together over Christmas. In the future. I'm starting to hope that we'll make this a thing—a real, real-life thing—and every time I think it I get this sinking feeling, like it's all too perfect to be true.

"That would be great!" I say, with genuine enthusiasm. "Does he always stay with you at Christmas?"

Aiden shakes his head. "Nah. But every few years or so. His parents spend a lot of time in the lodge and they like to

49

get away to the sun when they can, which is pretty much just Christmas and New Year. Dave's not into it - he's more of a White Christmas type - so he comes to stay with me or spends time with his sister Anna and her family." He wipes the corners of his mouth with his napkin, sets it down on the table and leans back in his chair, looking satisfied.

"Though, between you and me, Lexi has way more to do with him coming here than I do."

"Oh?" I say, brows lifting. I can feel myself leaning forward a little at this snippet.

"Yeah. He's been madly in love with her ever since he was sixteen. They had a thing one year at the lodge, but then she started Wirl and moved here and I guess it just fizzled out."

I try to think of them together and it doesn't make any sense. She's so pristinely put-together and professional, and Dave, while undeniably handsome, is so completely laid back and chill that it's hard to imagine them not driving each other crazy.

"Hmm," I say, and Aiden seems to catch the skeptical tone in my voice. He smiles.

"Yeah. I don't know either." He calls the server over to ask for the check and turns back to me.

"You want to go for a cocktail?" he asks, and then nods to my glass of sparkling water. "Or are you completely off alcohol?"

"I mean, I'm not teetotal for life or anything," I say. "But I've been on a bit of a health kick recently. Promised myself a full year of clean living. And I need to be at the studio early because the deadline is looming for that mermaid piece."

Aiden clasps his hands over his heart in mock pain. "I know when I'm being rejected," he says, grinning. "But at least let me drop you home in my cab."

I look at him, my eyes narrowing again. What's the point of refusing to give him my number if he has my address?

"I'll close my eyes when we get to your neighborhood," he

says, and holds his index finger and middle finger together, against the side of his forehead. "Scout's honor."

"It's three," I tell him. He gives me a quizzical look. "Three fingers."

He quickly flicks up another finger—his pinky, on purpose—and grins.

"Fine," I say, rolling my eyes theatrically. I live in an apartment building, anyway, so it's not like he's coming right to my door. At least, that's how I convince myself to let him into my life just that little bit further.

When the check arrives, he will not hear a single word of me paying anything toward it. I try to give him cash, I offer my card, and when he refuses both and I offer to Venmo him, he says: "I don't know what that is. I'm old," as he hands his card to the server.

"Besides," he says, as we stand to leave. "You're buying me lunch, remember? Friday."

"Bagels in the studio is hardly the same thing," I protest as he slips my coat over my shoulders.

"A meal is a meal, little Pip," he grins. He signs the slip with a flourish, pockets his card again, and we head outside to hail a cab.

AIDEN

December 13, 2018

I get home late on Thursday after picking up my dry cleaning, and unexpectedly find Lexi in my kitchen, pouring a cup of coffee. "Hey Lexi!" I call, teasingly. "Fancy seeing you here."

"Oh, hey!" she smiles, looking at me over her shoulder. "Sorry I didn't message you. I have a meeting on this side of town in the morning so I thought I'd come and stay here. Find out how you're getting on at the new office. Want a cup?" she asks, nodding to the coffee machine. "It's decaf."

I accept the drink, and we sit on high stools at the breakfast bar, sipping coffee late in the evening. I tell her about the new office, the mishaps and successes, the clients that have come with me, the clearly deluded clients that didn't, and the new clients I've gained through the merger.

"And Pippa?" she asks, when she's bored with listening to me talk about work.

I smile at her, and she grins, placing her coffee down on the counter.

"Oh, dear, Aiden. I do believe you *like* this one."

"What do you mean, this one?" I say. "This is the first woman I've dated since college."

It's technically true. There have been one-night stands, but nothing serious since Sophie.

"Darling," she says, affecting an overly dramatic tone. "Let me be dramatic!"

At least she's self-aware.

"She's great," I say, nodding. I'm smiling without meaning to. "Really great." I know she wants more. She's looking for titillating gossip from her younger brother's life. I'd usually indulge her, but with Pippa it's just... different. I want to keep it to myself and savor it. Every moment that I'm not with her is a moment wasted, and every moment that I am with her seems to pass in the blink of an eye.

"Oh, come ON," Lexi says, exasperated. "Give me something here."

"Well, I was thinking of inviting her over on Christmas day."

Lexi looks at me, open-mouthed. "Wow. Really?" she asks. "That's... pretty serious. Right?"

"Right," I nod. "But I don't want to scare her away," I say, slipping accidentally into the sort of over-sharing Lexi is hankering for. "She still hasn't given me her number, but it—"

"Wait, wait," says Lexi, flapping her hand at me. "Still no number?"

"I have three digits," I say. I sound almost defensive. "Long story. But it feels right. You know?"

"No, Aiden," she says, shaking her head. "I don't know. I don't remember what a real man smells like. My magazine is my baby and my lover and my best friend. Sad, isn't it?"

"Very," I agree, nodding. I try to keep a straight face, but when she looks over at me I crack a smile and Lexi bats a hand at my shoulder.

"Well, I don't see any harm in inviting her," she says, after a moment's thought.

"That's what I thought. It'll be you, me, Dave and her. And maybe her roomie, if they were planning to spend the day together. It's not like it'd be just the two of us pretending we're married or something."

"You met her roommate?" asks Lexi.

I shake my head. "No. But I'm gonna invite her, just in case."

"Well. Like I said, no harm in asking. I've got one of those blow-up beds at my place. I'll bring it here, just in case."

"Thanks, Sis," I say. Even the thought of having Pippa here with me on Christmas day fills me with excitement. The last time I felt this way about the holidays, I still believed in Santa Claus.

"Oh, I wanted to ask you a favor," I continue, getting up to refill the coffee machine. Lexi perks up immediately, a quizzical look passing across her face. I seldom ask her for favors. Partly because she always offers her help and organizes everything without being asked—whether you want her to or not—and partly because I can get most things I need without having to ask anyone.

"Go on," she says, intrigued, sliding her cup down the counter toward me. I refill both our drinks and sit down to explain. She listens quietly, sipping her coffee and nodding thoughtfully now and then. By the time I'm done explaining, Lexi has agreed to think about my idea and pitch it to her team tomorrow. My head is still buzzing when I collapse into my bed, and I'm still tossing and turning when the clock ticks over to 2 am.

Despite my lack of sleep, I practically skip out of the office at lunchtime on Friday. My car is already waiting, and the driver gives me a funny look as I whizz past him into the back seat, grinning broadly.

"Afternoon!" I say, when he gets into the front. I give him the address of Pippa's studio and sit back, looking out of the window. The excitement of seeing her again makes everything seem a little brighter, and I watch the world go by for the full twenty minutes it takes us to get there. Not even the irate honking of cab drivers can dampen my mood.

But Pippa can.

I tell the driver to come back in an hour and hop out of the car, closing the door behind me. The heavy metal door of the studio is slightly ajar when I get to it. I'm not sure if that means she's in there with a client or something, so I push it open quietly and head inside.

As I round into the main, open space of the building, I see her standing alone in front of a workbench. She's wearing her clay-stained baggy pants and a thick, figure-hugging pullover, and her hair is tied up in a high ponytail.

Being careful to be quiet, or at least quiet enough that the combined sound of the whirring space-heater and the low-volume radio disguise my steps on the concrete floor, I sneak up behind her and slide my arms around her waist.

"Hey, beautiful," I croon, beside her ear.

She sniffs.

"Hey!" she says.

It's a bit too enthusiastic, a bit fake, and her voice sounds thick with emotion. I spin her around, and I can feel my heart skip a beat when I see her face. It's all red and blotchy —she has clearly been crying, a lot. There are still tears running down her cheeks, and she bats at them angrily with her hand.

"What's wrong?" I ask, holding her by her upper arms and searching her face for answers.

"Sorry," she says, shaking her head.

"Stop apologizing and tell me what's wrong." I can hear that edge in my voice again, but I can't help it. Seeing her upset like this has caused my mind to narrow to a singular focus. The only thing I want in this moment is to find the source of her sadness and eliminate it. I want to wrap her in a hug and see her beautiful smile.

She doesn't seem to mind my tone. She lifts her right hand and hands me a crumpled bit of paper.

Pulling her into my chest and holding her there with one arm while she sniffles, I hold up the paper and read it.

Mr. Ling has passed away. Over a month ago, and nobody bothered to tell her. On top of that, his son—presumably one of the children who spent part of his life being fed and cared for by Pippa's grandmother—has inherited the building. He doesn't want to sell, the letter says, but he'll have to if it doesn't start making some money. So he's putting the rent up to market price. The new rent figure is astronomical, and not at all justified by the little brick box building—but it is justified by the location. And he can do it, because there's no written lease agreement in place. He could sell this place for a fortune, and that's probably his plan. Force out the struggling sculptor and sell to some commercial developer.

"Bastard," I angrily exclaim, unable to contain myself.

Pippa has gathered her composure a little and takes the letter back from me.

"Sorry, Pip," I say, smoothing her hair while I run over every possible solution in my mind. It's all on the up-and-up, legally speaking. He can charge her market rent as a new owner and there's not a damn thing she can do about it without any contract in place. I look around the studio at all the pieces, and I feel like my rage might burst out of my chest at any moment. The entire room is packed with things that sing of her.

"It's alright," she says, dabbing at her face with her sleeve.

I stop her, and wipe my thumbs underneath her watery eyes.

"I knew it was coming, one day. I guess I just hoped it wouldn't be today. Or tomorrow. I'm stupid to have no plan, really."

"We'll figure something out," I tell her. I pull her over to the small, battered old couch at the far side of the studio and we sit down together. She leans into me and stares across the room. I stroke her hair and listen to her breathing as it settles, trying to think of anything I can do to help. I could maybe buy the place, at a stretch, and give it to her, but I really think she'd hate that idea. She'd say it was a crazy plan —if she didn't run away screaming—and she'd be right, considering how little we know about each other. That's way too much pressure to put on a new relationship. Especially considering that all my liquid assets just got plowed into my equity buy-in, so it'd mean a mortgage. A big one. But there must be *something* I can do.

"Hey," she says after a while, pushing up from me and turning to look at my face. She's still a bit red and blotchy, but she's not crying anymore. That, at least, is a relief. "I got you a bagel." She smiles weakly. She leans down and digs around in her huge bag, pulling out a distinctly bagel-shaped package.

"So you did," I say, taking it from her. She's trying not to dwell, so I don't want to pull her back into thinking about the letter. Keeping my arm around her, I open the bagel on my lap, one-handed.

"Oooh," I say. "Green stuff!"

She laughs, her face cracking into a wide smile that lifts her rosy cheeks, and I feel relief flood my veins.

"It's avocado egg salad," she says, nudging me.

I take a bite and nod approvingly. As lumpy green paste goes it's not half bad, even if I would never in a million years have ordered it for myself.

"What are you having?" I ask, looking down at her as she watches me.

"Oh, nothing," she says. "I've been getting some pretty bad heartburn since we went to that barbecue place, so I'm just taking it easy. I had some peppermint tea."

"Are you ok?" I frown at her with concern.

"It's nothing," she says. "Just not used to it after months of green tea and salads."

I take another bite of my bagel and accept the bottle of water she offers me. "We'll have to get you used to the opulent life again," I say, watching for her reaction.

To my delight, the joke elicits one of her elusive secret smiles. She only gives that particular smile every so often, where the end of her nose crinkles a little and her dimple turns into a crater on her cheek, and I've convinced myself that she saves it just for me.

I make quick work of the rest of my bagel, and then we sit and chat. Inevitably, she brings the discussion back around to the letter. This time, however, she's much more practical about it, and much less distressed.

"...And I was only saying to you just the other day that maybe a place further out would be nice, wasn't I? I guess the rent would be a lot cheaper. Sure, I'd have to travel to see my friends, and you…"

She goes on, but I'm left dwelling on her statement that she'd have to travel to see me. If that's on her mind, then maybe she can see a future for us the same way I can. Which makes it even more important that I find a solution to Mr. Ling Jr's letter. I'm not sure I could stand by and watch her leave all over again.

"I have options, anyway," she says eventually.

"Yes, you do," I agree. I'm holding her hand, trailing the tip of my forefinger up and down as she talks. When she stops, I bring her hand to my mouth and kiss it. "You going to be alright if I go back to the office?" I ask.

She smiles and nods, looking much brighter than when I arrived.

"Yeah."

"Good," I say, with a decisive nod. I get to my feet and brush the bagel crumbs from my pants, then hold out my hand to help her up. "Where shall I pick you up tomorrow?"

"Tomorrow?" she asks, looking confused.

"Are you busy tomorrow?" I ask.

"Uh. No," she says, shaking her head. "I don't... think so? We didn't arrange anything, did we?"

"No," I reassure her. I lean down and kiss her forehead because I have to. Because she looks so fragile with her blotchy cheeks, but so strong with her shoulders pushed back, as though she's trying to force herself to face the world head-on. "But I'd like to take you out for the day. I need to do some Christmas shopping. You can be my guide, since you know the city. And I'll take you ice-skating to show my appreciation. There's nothing you can do about Ling until Monday, anyway. Sound good?"

I see her mind ticking over as I speak, and when I mention ice-skating she looks at me and grins. For just a moment, she looks like she hasn't a care in the world.

"Sounds good," she says. "You remember which street my apartment's on?"

"I do," I say, nodding.

"Okay, what time shall I come down?"

"Ten," I say, decisively.

"Ten, then," she says.

I lean down and kiss her on the mouth, gently at first, and then more deeply, pulling her closer to me. I can taste the salty tears lingering on her lips and smell a hint of peppermint on her breath.

"You're beautiful," I tell her, as we break apart. "See you tomorrow."

I turn to walk out, then stop.

"Here," I say, turning around. I reach into my pocket and fish around for a business card, forgetting that my new cards aren't back from the printers yet. I reach for my inside pocket instead and pull out a pen and a small notebook. I scribble down my number and hand it to her.

"You don't have to look at it," I tell her, a somber look on my face. "I just want to know that you have it. In case you need me. Any time, alright?"

She glances at the paper and her lips twitch with a smile.

"Thank you," she says, quietly pocketing the paper.

I kiss her forehead one last time and head out, reluctantly, to the waiting car. It's only now that I glance at my watch and realize that the driver has been waiting for thirty minutes, and I have a meeting soon. A meeting, I realize with a touch of surprise, that I would have gladly canceled in a heartbeat if she'd asked me to stay. I had fully intended to ask her to join me for Christmas today, but now that will have to wait.

"Afternoon!" says the driver. He sounds chipper, but I can't tell if it's sarcasm.

I give him a curt, apologetic nod, and climb in.

PIPPA

December 15, 2018

When my alarm goes off on Saturday morning at 8 am, I peel my eyes open groggily and stare at the ceiling above my bed. Ten whole, blissful seconds pass before I remember Ling's letter. In a matter of weeks or months, I'm likely to have no studio to work in. I grab my pillow from behind my head and hold it over my face. Petulantly, I lift my legs and kick them back down into my mattress repeatedly, screaming into the pillow. Though I'm slightly embarrassed to admit it, this little tantrum actually does make me feel a bit better, like some of the tension I've been carrying since yesterday morning has been eased out of me.

Don't get me wrong, it was great to talk to Aiden about it, and he was really supportive. But Valerie was out for some Christmas drinks with family friends last night and won't be back until tomorrow. Usually I'd have poured out my heart to her and listened to her calling Mr. Ling every name under the sun, but instead, I've been left inside my own head, and all it seems able to do is worry.

I'm debating whether to roll out of bed onto the floor and crawl to the kitchen to get some tea, when I remember why my alarm clock is going off on Saturday.

"Aiden!" I say out loud, sitting bolt upright in the bed. My heart is suddenly soaring, and even the weight of Ling's threats can't keep it down.

Within a couple of minutes, I'm standing in the shower, letting the hot water run down over my back as I brush my teeth and think about the day ahead. I try not to let my imagination run away with me, but things have been going so well since we met again. It's been less than a week and I already feel like there's this unspoken agreement that we'll see each other regularly. If I can stop crying all over him all the time, maybe we'll actually make something of this thing. It feels so strange now that I held back from getting involved with him, especially since the heartbreak I felt after that week in the snow was far heavier than any I'd felt before it.

When I'm dried and my hair is pulled up into a messy bun that takes me almost half an hour to get right, I pull on a pair of blue skinny jeans with brown, knee-high boots, and select a chunky, cream-coloured pullover with an asymmetrical off-shoulder collar. It's not the most practical thing to wear in the middle of winter, but I'm already smirking at all the "cold shoulder" jokes I can make, and I really don't hate what I'm seeing in the mirror.

I stand there for a couple of minutes, turning this way and that, and it's long enough that the press of the waistband against my tummy becomes uncomfortable. I dig a pair of jeggings out of the darkest recesses of my closet and put them on instead of jeans. They don't look quite as good as the jeans, but at least I can move in them. Since there was mention of ice skating, I consider that a win.

By the time I'm done putting on my makeup, it's 9:15 am.

I have enough time to make tea and eat breakfast, so I put a couple of eggs on the stove, some bread in the toaster, and flick on the TV.

I almost drop my tea when I look up and see Lexi on the screen, in all her pristine glory, sitting elegantly on a couch in some TV studio and smiling to the hosts. I grab the remote to turn up the volume. It's some sort of weekend breakfast show, and they're talking about her magazine.

"And after all that struggle and hard work, you now find yourself right at the top," says one of the hosts. "More traffic than any of your competitors last month, some of the biggest celebrity interviews of recent years under your belt, and you're favourite to be voted E-zine of the Year at the end of the month. How does it feel?"

"Damn," I say, realizing I've missed most of the interview.

"Wonderful, of course," says Lexi. Her smile is warm and humble, and she looks every bit the consummate professional. "I could never have dreamed of all this when I started out blogging from my bedroom all those years ago. But I'm never satisfied. All of our readers should look forward to bigger and better things next year!"

"There you have it, folks," says the other host, looking to the camera. "The wonderful Lexi Coleman."

He goes on to talk about the next feature. Something about the perfect makeup tips for this season's parties, but I'm not listening.

"Coleman," I say, feeling the word in my mouth. That's probably Aiden's last name, too. "Coleman," I say again, lingering my tongue around the back of my teeth. I reach for my laptop to unleash my meager web searching skills, but then I hesitate. That week in March was so perfect, and things with Aiden are so good now, that I don't want to find out anything that would bring it all crashing down. But if there is something I should know, wouldn't it be better to know now? Just as I'm about to really get into an argument with myself, the egg timer pings and the toast pops up from the toaster. I take it as a sign from the universe, leave my laptop where it is, and spend the next half an hour watching strangers paint other strangers while I eat my breakfast.

I hear a horn honk outside at exactly 10 am, and when I lean over to look out the window, I see Aiden standing outside a black car, looking up with a squint against the morning sky. I quickly wipe the corners of my mouth and drain the last of my tea. I brush the crumbs from my lap, grab my purse and coat, and head down.

As I head out into the frosty morning, I'm surprised to see that Aiden is not driving himself. Instead I'm greeted by a driver in an expensive suit, who walks around the car and opens the back door for me to get in. I don't know what sort of car it is, but I know it's fancy. And I'm getting the distinct feeling that Aiden is a little further along the career path than Valerie, with her subway tickets and ridiculously long hours. I'd probably find all this off-putting if I didn't like him so much already.

When I slide into the back seat, Aiden is sitting there in all his glory, smiling at me. He looks more like Aiden from the lodge in his sweater and jeans. Gorgeous from head to toe. I can see his eyes working their way down my body and back up, taking in the outfit I've picked. His gaze lingers on my face. If anyone else inspected me like this, I'd probably collapse in on myself, but Aiden manages to make me feel beautiful with a glance.

"Hey, Pip," he says, and as I settle nervously into the seat, he reaches over, grabs my wrist, and tugs me towards him. The fact that he does this and doesn't seem to care that his driver is there gives me a little thrill. He leans down to kiss me on my lips, and I feel sparks of electricity where our bodies touch.

"Hey, yourself," I say. I'm smiling at him so wide I can feel the tension in my cheeks. "I just saw Lexi on the TV!" I tell him as he tucks me under his arm. The warmth of his body envelopes me.

"Ah, yeah. She does that a lot. It's hard, you know? Being the downtrodden, nobody brother of such a superstar."

I hear the sarcasm in his voice before I look up to see his grin.

"I mean," I say. "You don't seem to be doing too bad yourself. Unless you stole this car... and the driver?"

"You got me," he says, his hands coming up in surrender. He reaches forward and pushes a small button on the arm rest. "Isn't that right, Dev?" he says.

"Sir?" comes the driver's voice, tinny and electric through the car's intercom. I see his eye flick up to the rear-view, and focus briefly on me, then on Aiden.

"I was just telling Pippa here that I stole the car and kidnapped you. You live in dire circumstances now, isn't that right?"

"That's right, Sir," says Dev, looking to me in the mirror and nodding. I can see crinkles at the corners of his eyes that give away his smile, and then the crackly background sound of the intercom is gone.

"See?" says Aiden, looking at me as I shake my head, chuckling. "I'm a bad man."

"Well, I was never in any doubt about that," I say, snuggling in to his side.

"Dev just arrived from Boston," he explains. "He's been my driver there for a few years and it worked really well, so I asked him to join me here."

I look back up at the rear-view, but Dev's eyes are on the road and his expression is neutral. I'm a little impressed, I admit, that Aiden has apparently inspired such loyalty in his driver that he's uprooted his life to continue working for him.

"So what's the plan?" I ask.

"Shopping," he says, without hesitation. "And ice skating. And food. That alright?"

I nod.

"I need to get something for Lexi," he says. "Something special, because she's been so good, helping me with the move from Boston. But she's so hard to buy for, be—"

"Because she has everything?" I interject.

"You'd think," he says, shrugging, "but no. I mean sure, she does have everything. Everything she needs, anyway. But gifts for her are hard because she's just not about the money, you know? She can buy herself whatever she wants. She values sentimental gifts over anything. Thoughtful things. Something she can open and it'll bring a smile to her face because it will remind her of a memory we shared or a conversation we had."

I consider this for a moment. I liked Lexi from the moment I found out she wasn't Aiden's date, but I definitely made some assumptions about her - the fashion-first, glamorous, maybe slightly superficial It Girl - that are being challenged by this conversation, and I'm a little embarrassed that I jumped to those conclusions based on nothing more than her killer outfits. I quietly resolve not to make that mistake again.

Outside, the Christmas lights and decorations pass in a blur, before we hit city traffic and slow down. I swear I spot ten Santas every block, each surrounded by at least a dozen children clamoring to tell him their deepest wishes for Christmas morning.

"So what sort of things have you got her before?" I ask, eventually.

"Well, I guess I should tell you about the original and best," he says, pulling me in a little closer, like it's story time.

"When we were kids—I was about eight, so she would have been ten—we were at the ski lodge a bit before Christmas. Lexi, Dave, Anna and I were messing about just off the

66

slopes, throwing snowballs and all. Dave threw a big one over at Lexi and she lost her footing and fell over, rolled down the hill and ended up colliding awkwardly with a tree."

"Oh, no!" I say. "Was she alright?" I'm enjoying the glimpse into his past. I can still feel the worry of potentially losing the studio, lingering there under the surface, but I've resolved to let myself relax today, to try to forget about it and just enjoy myself. And that seems to be Aiden's plan as well.

"She was alright. No serious injuries, but she'd fractured some important little bone in her elbow. So they had her in a cast from her hand to her shoulder, all through Christmas."

"Man, that must have sucked."

"Yeah. So anyway, I bought her a Barbie doll and Dave, Anna and I spent hours one day making papier mâché and giving this doll a matching cast to Lexi's. Man, she was so stoked when she opened it. Seriously, her face lit up like nothing I've ever seen."

"Aww, that's really cute," I say, looking up at him. He's grinning from the memory, and his cheeks are pitted with gorgeous dimples.

"Yep. And I mean, this was a girl who had the biggest collection of Barbie dolls you've ever seen. But broken arm Barbie was her instant favourite. And since then, I try to get her something meaningful for Christmas."

"Any idea what you're going to get her this year?"

"Nope!" he says, shaking his head. "Not a damn clue. And I have Dave to buy for, too, but he's much easier. Some techy gadget will please him well enough."

"So it's just the three of you on Christmas day? At your place, or at Lexi's?" I ask.

There's a moment of silence and I look up to see him staring over the top of my head and out of the window with a blank expression on his face.

"Aiden?"

"Hmm?" he asks. And then he seems to be back in the car

with me all of a sudden. "Oh, yeah," he says, nodding. His smile comes a little slow, making me wonder what he was thinking about, but I let it go and nod.

We spend the rest of the journey in relative silence. I assume he's racking his brain to try to come up with the perfect gift for Lexi, and I'm more than happy to stay tucked under his arm, pressed against his firm body, watching the seasonal city roll by outside.

"I'll call later, Dev," says Aiden, when we reach our destination. "Take some chill time. I've got the doors."

Dev nods in the rearview, and Aiden slips his arm from around my shoulders to get out. I scoot over, about to follow him, when suddenly the door slams shut a couple of inches from my face. I can feel the slack-jaw expression on my face, and my shocked brain is trying to decide which expletive I should yell first, but a moment later the door on my side opens, and I see Aiden standing there, holding out his hand to help me out of the car. I feel a flush of embarrassment rising up under my coat as I reach for his hand and pull myself out. Dev probably thinks I'm an idiot, but I'm too wrapped up in the magic of being treated so chivalrously to give it much thought.

Despite the daylight, Madison Avenue is glittering from start to finish. There are throngs of shoppers hurrying up and down, rushing in and out of stores and coffeehouses, and I can hear three different Christmas songs at once, all competing for the attention of gift-hunters. Aiden takes my hand and slips my arm into the crook of his elbow, and as we walk down the street the city stench of traffic fumes gradually gives way to a lighter, almost sickly scent of cinnamon and coffee.

We visit no less than seven stores within an hour, and I'm shocked at how efficient Aiden is. He has a task to complete, and he is *on it*. I walk along beside him, happy to observe him in action as he strides through crowds that seem to part for him, scanning every shelf and aisle for anything of interest. He stops a couple of times, picking up and quickly replacing a few things that I imagine were possible gifts for Dave. We linger the longest in a joke shop, and draw the attention of other shoppers with our laughing as we try out prosthetic noses and fart machines.

An hour of browsing later, it's time for lunch. I can feel my feet swelling inside my boots, and I visibly wince when I step on an uneven paving stone.

"What?" Aiden demands, stopping dead in his tracks and turning to me. A squat man nearly walks dead into Aiden and mutters a curse, but when he looks up and sees Aiden staring down at him, he meekly side-steps and continues on his way.

"Nothing," I say, trying to smile brightly.

"You're really a terrible liar," he says, smiling. He places a finger under my chin and tips it up. I love it when he does that. I'm instantly tingling all over.

"My feet. They've been getting a bit sore lately," I tell him. "It's nothing."

He glances down at my feet, holding my upper arms with his hands, then lifts his gaze to my face again. He looks way more concerned about my swollen feet than I am.

"Lately?" he asks.

"Couple of months."

"Seen a doctor?"

I shake my head. "Figured I'd go after Christmas."

"If the New Year rolls around and you still haven't been, I'm going to make you an appointment and take you to it. Alright?" he says.

I lift my brows. He has a way of being so demanding sometimes, but it never makes me feel condescended to. I feel... cared for.

"Yes, boss," I say, sarcastically, and salute.

"Good," he says, and his thumb moves up a little from my

chin to swipe ever so gently over my bottom lip. The sudden roll of desire that wells up inside me is almost overwhelming. "Good," he says again, and I notice his Adam's apple bob as he swallows. "Now, let's get some lunch. We'll skip skating if your feet are hurting."

"But I was going to show off!" I whine.

He looks at me with narrowed eyes. "Oh were you, now? How's that?"

"I *might* have done some figure skating when I was younger," I tell him, looking around innocently.

"Ah, so you're a hustler!" he says, laughing, and offers me his arm again, which I gladly take. "Well, maybe next year."

I'm speechless for a moment, trying to parse what he means by next year. Next Christmas? Next year in a few weeks' time? It's hard to deny that I'm starting to fall for him, big time. And I'm struggling to find any reason not to.

AIDEN

I can't shake the worry about her feet. It's been nearly a decade since Sophie first started complaining of niggling little pains and aches, but the horror is still with me. I could never go through that again. I'm trying to walk slowly so that Pippa will be able to keep up, but the instinct to run away from the worry is almost too much. I try to slow my breathing and calm myself, reassure myself that it's not the same, and that I don't need to worry about losing Pip the same way.

I've just about managed to push it out of my mind when we happen upon a diner, and step inside to grab some lunch.

"Wow, this place is... festive," says Pippa.

She's not wrong. There are gold, red and silver streamers hanging from every inch of the ceiling, a peppy, rock-beat version of Jingle Bells is playing a little too loud, and the servers are all dressed as elves—striped tights and all.

"No kidding," I say, guiding her into an empty booth.

We order some drinks—a beer for me and sparkling water for her—and sit in silence to look at the menu. I can't help looking over at her as she sits there, studying the menu as if this is the most important decision she's ever made.

She's beautiful. Not in an obvious, supermodel sort of way, but in an effortless, natural sort of way. Something has changed, since March. I don't know if she's lost a little weight or gained a little weight, or if it's just the effect of time and longing, but she looks more beautiful to me today than ever before.

"Ready?" asks the server, suddenly appearing beside me. I look across to Pippa, who's nodding.

"Alright, then," I say. "Ladies first!"

I would have said that anyway, but I'm a little relieved to have some time to quickly pick something out while she's ordering. She gets the cob salad and I end up ordering the same. The server takes the menus and heads off with our order, and Pippa looks over to me and smiles.

"So," she says.

"So," I repeat. "Feet better?"

"Yeah. Much better, thanks. It's nothing major. Probably the boots. Hey, we didn't get anything for Lexi and Dave yet."

"I'll come in again another time," I tell her. "I'm not dragging you around on sore feet. What sort of monster do you think I am?"

"Aside from a kidnapper and grand theft... auto-ist? Well that would be telling, Mr. Coleman," she says, and I narrow my eyes at her. She's been doing some detective work.

"Quite so, Ms. Holmes," I say, and she laughs. It splits the air like glitter, brightening up the atmosphere in an instant.

"I saw Lexi's name on the TV this morning and just assumed..."

"Ah," I say, nodding. "So you haven't Googled me yet, then?"

"No," she says, shaking her head. "I mean, I was going to, but then they started telling me how to apply this season's hot new eye makeup and I couldn't drag myself away."

I think I love her.

It dawns on me in that instant, and it's the most ridiculous thought I've ever had. I've known her for all of two weeks, and one of those was a no-strings-attached vacation fling. And aside from all that, I know how much it hurts when it all goes terribly wrong. And yet, here I am, thinking it, regardless.

I must be looking at her strangely, because she tilts her head and gives me a puzzled expression.

"You okay?" she asks.

"Yeah," I say, trying to sound breezier than I feel. The server comes along to deliver our drinks, saving me from the moment.

"Yeah, just glad you've got your priorities straight," I say, recovering myself. "Eye makeup first, always."

"Hear, hear," she laughs, and lifts up her glass. We clink, and takes simultaneous sips.

"So, hey," she says, looking at me across the table. There's a little pink flush in her cheeks. "What's the deal with Lexi? I mean. She's not married or dating, right? Is she just a workaholic? Sorry to pry, it's just... she's so nice and so beautiful..."

I smile at her, as gently as I can, and shake my head. "You're not prying. It's a perfectly normal thing to wonder. And it's something like that, I guess. Partly, she's just really busy with work all the time. And partly... well, I think the main problem is that nobody she ever meets is Dave."

"Dave Dave?" she asks as she leans in closer. She looks comical in her sudden interest. "That's right, you mentioned they had a thing."

"Dave Dave," I nod. "Dave Driscoll. They're made for each other. But she has her career here in the city and he's a country boy through-and-through. They dated for a while, but—"

"Really?! I thought you just meant a one-night stand or something."

I laugh at the look on her face. It's true that Dave and Lexi

73

seem like polar opposites when you meet them. And in many ways, they are. Pippa's shock is understandable.

"Yep. Back when they were in their late teens. I know it's hard to imagine, but that's because you've never seen them together. They got on like a house on fire, but Dave was about to start college, Lexi was already in college on the other side of the country, and vacations just weren't enough. And I think the two of them sort of realized they were on different paths. It's a shame, really."

"Yeah," she says, nodding. "And what about you?"

I look up sharply at her—more sharply than I want to.

"Sorry," she says. "I didn't mean to pry." There's a look of embarrassment on her face that makes me want to hug her. I reach across the table and take her hand.

"It's fine. I dated a little in college. There was someone serious, but it ended. And then I got busy with work. And then I met you."

I left a lot out there. I didn't mention Sophie by name, nor that I'd planned to be with her forever. I didn't mention the way it ended, or why, or how much it messed me up. Just the basics. But that will have to do.

"Short but sweet," she says, looking satisfied. She's obvious realized I'm not up for talking about it and she's willing to let it slide.

"Just like you!" I say, grinning at her, and she throws a napkin at me.

The food is surprisingly good, considering that the only reason we're in here is it was the first place we came across. In the middle of eating, I get an idea for something we can do instead of ice-skating. I'm not ready to let the day end halfway through, so I ask her to excuse me for a moment, and fire off a quick text to Dev.

Thank heavens Dev agreed to move to the Big Apple - at a significantly higher rate, of course. The company guy that's been driving me around since I got here is fine, but Dev has been with me for years, we each know how the other works, and he goes above and beyond. Now that he's relocated, New York City is beginning to feel a bit more permanent.

Pippa and I chat a little about what I might get for Lexi and Dave for Christmas, and she says she needs to pick something out for her mother and her roommate.

"Well, when I do eventually find gifts for them," I say, "you want to come see their reactions when they open them?"

She pauses in the middle of wiping her mouth and looks over at me.

"What?" she asks.

Admittedly, it's not the big speech I thought I'd be making, about how much I like her and how I want her to come and be with me, but trying to come up with the right words has been freaking me out, and this feels more natural.

"Spend Christmas with me," I say. "With us. At my place."

"I…" She looks speechless. There's a sudden, sinking lurch in my stomach, and for a second I think I've blown it.

"I mean if you're already busy, it's fine," I say, quickly.

"No, no. It's not that," she says, shaking her head. "Well, it sort of is. My mother is going away for Christmas and my roomie and I were going to have a girly Christmas at the apartment, watching old-time movies and pigging out on ice-cream."

She grins, and so do I—but I'm not willing to let it go just yet.

"Bring her along?" I say. "It makes sense, no? There'd be five of us altogether. You can't even play charades with two!"

"Or three," she says, accusingly.

"Or three," I agree. "So let's save charades. Together."

She laughs at this, and I feel relief flooding me.

"I'll have to ask," she says, but I can see her mind ticking over and the little smile tugging at her lips that says she wants to. Even if we can't pull it off, that smile is enough to keep me floating.

"Great," I say, lifting my now-empty glass. "To charades!"

The server comes along to clear our table, I win an argument with Pippa about who's going to pay, and while she pulls her coat on, I check my phone and see a message from Dev.

"Okay," I tell Pippa, taking her hand to lead her back into the street. "I'm not letting you stomp all over the city and pretend your feet are fine. Ice skating is out of the question. I can get the gifts I need next week, anyway. So we'll do something else."

She looks up at me, her huge, blue eyes questioning, with a curious look on her face. Thousands of Christmas lights give her eyes a shifting sparkle. "What are we doing?" she asks.

"You'll see," I tell her. I know there's going to be protest and questions before I say it, so I take the opportunity to lean down and press my lips against hers. Her hand lifts to sit flat upon my chest, and I cup the back of her head. Her lips are the softest, most yielding I've ever felt. I feel like I could stay in that kiss forever, until we're jostled a little too much by passing shoppers. Our teeth clonk together and we both break apart, laughing.

These are the moments I savor with her. It's not just that she's beautiful and soft and smoking hot. She has an edge to her. An incredible sense of humor, an easy-going attitude, artistic talent. She's so much more than a vacation fling, and I can no longer believe I agreed to that ridiculous arrangement in the first place.

"Ah, there he is," I say, nodding to the car that's just pulled in. Dev gets out and opens the back door, and we hop in.

"Mystery tour!" Pippa grins, as I get in and sit beside her.

I tease her about where we're going. The mountains. The ski slope. The North Pole. She doesn't believe any of it, but I manage to make her laugh, and I get to see her dimples.

Less than ten minutes later, we're pulling up near Central

Park, and Dev once again gets out to open the sidewalk-side door.

"Thanks, man," I say to him, quietly, as he slips a piece of paper into my hand. "Call you later."

When Dev is back in the car, I turn to Pippa and offer her my arm.

"Sooo… a walk in Central Park?" she asks, and I'm loving the way she's so desperate to know. I give her a sly side-smile and she gives me a frustrated little grunt in return.

"You think I'd drag you around Central Park after you've told me your feet are sore?" I ask her.

"Hmm," she says. "No, I don't."

"Well, you'd be wrong," I tell her, grinning. I nod over her shoulder, and she turns around to see a small, horse-drawn carriage sitting at the side of the path. It's my surprise to her, but even I'm impressed by how pretty and romantic it looks. There are glittering fairy lights wrapped around its edges, and the seats are covered in deep-red velvet cushions.

"Seriously?" she says, turning back around to face me. Her face is bright with excitement. She looks like a kid on Christmas morning, and I instantly know I've made the right choice.

"Coleman?" says a short, wiry man with a friendly face, as he emerges from behind the horse, giving it a quick rub on the nose.

"That's us," I nod, and I hold my arm out, indicating Pippa should go first.

"Now, once we've got you settled in under a nice cozy blanket, we'll do the full tour," says the man. "Frank's the name, by the way. We'll stop now and then at the landmarks, but if you want to get out you just let me know."

He holds out a hand to help Pippa up into the carriage, and I pull out the ticket that Dev handed me, passing it off to Frank.

"All aboard," he says, when I've pulled myself up and settled in beside Pippa.

She immediately grabs the blanket from the opposite seat and pull it over us, wriggling into my side.

"I've never been in one of these!" she says, excitedly, all dimples and delight. "I've lived here almost my entire life and barely ever been in Central Park. Strange, isn't it, how people come from all over the world to see the sights of the place you live in, and you barely even notice them when they're right in front of you?"

I nod, draping my arm over her shoulder and sitting back. "Sometimes, you don't know what you've got until someone points it out to you. Or until you lose it."

I don't feel the usual pang of guilt when I talk about losing love, and its absence is so shocking it almost feels like a part of me is missing.

She looks up at me, meaningfully, her teeth pressed into her bottom lip. "Maybe people should be more careful about keeping the things they hold dear close by," she says. "And not let them go because of some stupid agreement they made on the spur of the moment."

"What sort of idiots would do that?" I ask, playing along, but my heart is pounding in my chest as she grins back at me. That must mean what I think it means, right? I swoop down to kiss her, but she's barely parted her lips when Frank's voice interrupts us.

"Off we go!"

The carriage jerks a little as it starts into motion, and then the ride is slow and smooth.

"Aww, that could've been us," says Pippa, as we pass by the Wollman Rink.

"Pfft. Yeah, and I'd have been on my ass with bruises while you glided round like a swan," I snort. I squeeze her a little tighter into my side. "This is much better."

On we go, past the carousel that's bustling with families

and couples. We ride by the glittering Plaza Hotel and along the Upper East Side, its looming buildings painting an old-style silhouette against the grey, cloudy sky. Frank gives us some landmark commentary here and there. Pippa's eyes are wide as she looks around, taking it all in like a tourist in her own city, and the cold in the air has made her nose and cheeks bright pink. She looks adorable.

"Oh! Frank…" she says. Frank half-turns his head to hear. "Frank, can we stop here?"

"Woah, boy!" Frank calls to the horse, and I glance around as the carriage draws to a slow halt, wondering why she's asking to stop here. By the time I turn back to look at her, she's already out of the carriage.

"Come on!" she says, turning her head to look at me over her shoulder. She's grinning and beckoning me with her hand. Beyond her, I can see some sort of statue.

"It's Balto," she says, as I draw nearer to her. She reaches out for my hand and I gladly offer it, looking up at the image of a big dog, perched high up on a rock.

"Man, I forgot this was here," she says, looking up at me with her eyes gleaming. "My mother brought me here when I was a kid. I can still remember it so clearly. She told me about the husky, Balto, and how he led a dog sled team through a blizzard to deliver a serum that saved hundreds of people from some sort of epidemic. And then he was immortalized here. It was the first time I ever realized that making things like this was something that people did. For a job."

"This your favourite statue?" I ask her, looking up at Balto.

"No," she says, immediately, shaking her head. "I'm not sure I have a favourite, but this has a special place in my heart. It's by Frederick Roth. He was really incredible at capturing motion. See how he's standing?" she asks me.

I look up again, and sure enough, she's right. Balto looks

like he's about to bark and leap down from the rock at any second.

"He studied fine art and animals," she says, as I gaze upward. "Some of his smaller works are amazing, too."

She leans into me, and I'm happy to stand there, looking up at Balto in silence with her, while the warmth of her small form seeps into me through the thick mass of coats between us. We only move when Frank clears his throat behind us, signalling that it's time to move on.

Once we're back in the carriage, we carry on our tour. The park is all lit up and twinkling, and there are plenty of people out enjoying the crisp, winter air, or rushing through with bags full of shopping. We pass by the boat pond, and, soon enough, we're riding by Bethesda Fountain. Pippa tells me about the statue atop it, *The Angel of the Waters*, and about the woman who sculpted it, Emma Stebbins, who was the first woman ever to receive a public art commission from New York City. A trailblazer. It's enthralling, how much she knows about her craft and how passionate she is about it.

We ride along the Upper West Side, past Strawberry Fields and Sheep Meadow and a playground full of children in mittens and hats, and eventually, when it's drawing close to evening, we arrive back where we began.

After thanking Frank for the ride, we walk down the street arm in arm. To say that I'm not eager for the day to end would be an understatement. I spent almost every second of that week in the ski lodge beguiled by this woman, and now I find myself in the same situation again—and then some. That week in March was mostly sex and laughter, and awkwardly avoiding any mention of our real lives to each other. The more I get to know about her out here in the world, the more I want to have her forever, every moment, every day.

"You want to come to my place?" I ask.

She seems genuinely regretful when she looks up at me.

"I'd love to come to your place, but the deadline for the mermaid is looming. If I'm going to spend Christmas with you, I really need to get some work done on it tomorrow."

I'm disappointed, but I know deadlines better than most people. If anything, I admire her commitment.

"I understand." I tell her. "And I'm up to my neck in meetings this week, so I'm not going to be able to see you until Christmas. Which means it's going to drag."

This news seems to irk her as much as it irks me, which softens the blow a bit. She sighs a resigned little sigh.

"A farewell coffee, then?" she asks, nodding across the street to a coffeehouse.

I smile at her and nod, and we head in that direction. Just as we get to the other side of the street, I hear her gasp. I look down, and she's holding her gloved hand up to me.

"Look!" she says.

There, on her glove, is a rapidly melting little snowflake. We both look up together to see a sparse shower of snow falling from the sky.

"It's going to be a white Christmas!" she says, grinning up at me.

We end up staying in the coffeehouse for a few hours, sipping different teas and chatting. The warm cups do our frozen fingers the world of good, and by the time I drop her off back at her apartment, it's long since dark. She gives me a lingering kiss, needy and passionate and soft at once.

As she goes to get out of the door that Dev is holding open, I grab her wrist. "Pippa," I say. She turns to look at me, that secret little smile sparkling in her eyes.

"I need to get a Christmas tree. On Christmas Eve. Come with me?"

A smile blooms on her face and she nods. "Sure, hot stuff. Pick me up at the studio."

I pull her back to peck another quick kiss to her lips, and let her go.

PIPPA

December 17, 2018

B y the time Monday rolls around, I'm really starting to miss Aiden. Saturday in the city was magical, even if we didn't end up ice-skating. Or buying any gifts. Or doing anything we'd planned to, really. The tour of Central Park really reminded me how great this city is and how many gems it hides in its busy streets. Which would all be fine, if it didn't make me even more fretful about losing the studio and having to look for something further out. Fortunately, I've been able to throw myself into work and mostly forget about it.

The mermaid is looking much more mermaidy by the time my tummy gives a loud rumble and I look up at the clock. It's 3 pm and I haven't eaten since breakfast, so I wipe the excess clay off my hands and sit down on the battered old couch to eat my turkey sandwich. I've just taken the very first bite, when there's a loud banging at the studio door. Sighing around a cheekful of half-masticated crust, I put my sandwich down on the arm of the couch and get up to answer the door.

"Heeey, Pippa!"

It's Lexi, standing in the snow, smiling and waving at me, looking as perfectly put-together as ever.

"Sorry to drop by like this, but I had a meeting canceled, so I thought I'd slot you in now, if that's alright?"

I can feel myself staring at her, and I know that my face looks strange. One of my cheeks is bulging out with the turkey sandwich inside it, and my eyes are wide like saucers. She was the last person I expected to see. Realising I'm being rude, I swallow in one big gulp and smile at her. Purely out of habit, I wipe my hands down the front of my clay-smeared coveralls and hold one out to help her in from the snow.

"Sorry," I say, once we're safely inside and the door is closed. I lead her through to the main studio where the quiet hum of an electric heater is the only sound. "I wasn't expecting anyone. Did we have an appointment? Aiden didn't mention anything…" I trail off, and watch her as her eyes start to flit here and there in the studio, first to the almost-mermaid in the middle of the room, and then around at the other completed pieces I have displayed around the perimeter.

"Hm?" she says, looking back to me. "Oh, no, darling. Sorry, I should have explained myself properly. Shall we sit?" she asks, looking over at the threadbare couch.

"Oh lord, did I interrupt your lunch?" she asks, noticing the sandwich sitting on the arm of the couch. "Please, don't put it off on my account. Eat up."

She's not rude or domineering, but she's definitely type A. Within seconds, I'm being led to the couch in my own studio, and sitting down while someone I wasn't expecting starts conducting a meeting.

"The thing is," she begins, placing her purse on her lap. She picks up my sandwich and hands it to me, and I take it without thinking. Too curious about why she's here to protest or actually do anything with it, I hold it in my hand, and listen. "Well, Aiden told me about your work. And I have to agree with him, even just on first glance. There's some stunning stuff here, Pippa."

She's smiling warmly, and I can feel myself smiling back. I'm proud of what I've made in this studio, and of the commissioned pieces that have found their home elsewhere.

"Thank you," I say, hoping I'm not blushing too much.

"I want to run a profile piece on you," she says.

I can feel my brows raise almost to my hairline, and I don't know what to say.

"On me?" is what my brain comes up with.

"Well, it'll be a series," she says. "I've been planning it for a while. Artists of New York City, showcasing a different high-talent, low-profile artist every week. When Aiden mentioned that you're a sculptor and that he loved your work, I just knew it was fate."

"Wow," I breathe. I really don't know what to say. Lexi's magazine is one of the biggest in the country. I can barely begin to imagine what that sort of exposure would do for me. It's an artists dream, for sure, but I'm so blindsided by it I can't find the right reaction.

Lexi must be used to this sort of thing, because she sits there, patiently, waiting for it to sink in a bit, before she goes on.

"I'd need to bring a photographer here. And arrange a proper appointment with you for an interview. Aiden says you're on a tight deadline at the moment with the mermaid," she says, looking over at it. "Beautiful piece, by the way. So... are you in?"

Whatever trouble my brain is having connecting with my mouth, it doesn't have the same issue with my head. I nod a few times, and then my mouth catches up.

"Yeah! Yes. I mean, wow, Lexi. That would be great, but…" my brow furrows.

"It's nothing to do with you and Aiden being an item," she says, as though reading my mind. "He's just how I found you. I'd be here if it was anyone else whose opinion I trusted, too. So put that out of your mind."

I can see how she got as far as she has. She's perceptive and sharp and confident. I smile at her, even if the smallest bit of my mind is still lingering on the fact that she called Aiden and I "an item".

"Alright then," I nod. "Great. Thank you. I could really use this. More than you know."

"The studio?" Lexi asks. "Sorry. Aiden just mentioned something about it after he'd seen you one day. He was so mad. Will you let me look into it for you?"

"Uh, sure," I say, figuring that whatever can be done to try to help me stay here is worth a shot. I doubt I have a leg to stand on, given that there's no actual lease or contract, but I'm not quite ready to accept the inevitable yet.

"Great," says Lexi. "Awesome." And then there's a minor shift in her demeanor, almost imperceptible. Her shoulders drop maybe a half-inch and she leans back, and professional Lexi is suddenly replaced by personal Lexi. "Aiden says you're coming to us for Christmas," she says. "I was so thrilled to hear it. And I'm so glad you found him. Or he found you. Or however that happened. He was unbearable for months after he met you at the lodge."

"Really?" I ask, leaning forward. The sandwich is still in my hand. The parts that are in contact with my fingers are starting to get sticky.

"Mmhmm," she says, nodding. "He told me about your agreement, and I told him he was an idiot to go along with it. But I guess everything worked out. I haven't seen him this happy since…" she hesitated. "Well. A long time."

"The serious girl in college?" I ask, desperate for more

information about Aiden from someone who knows him so well.

Lexi nods, and there's something sad about the upturn of her lips that makes it not quite a smile. "Yes. Sophie," she says. "I'm surprised he mentioned her to you. He still finds it painful, even after all these years."

I frown, trying to imagine what sort of hellish breakup it could have been to still be affecting him. "Was she awful to him?" I ask, already feeling mad at whoever Sophie is for having hurt Aiden.

"Oh, no, Pippa. No, no. She was wonderful to him. They got together when they were nineteen. Second year of college. Everything was great, at first. They got on like a house on fire. She came and met our parents, he went and met hers. They were completely smitten with each other."

"What happened?" I ask, confused by how fondly Lexi speaks of the woman who'd obviously broken her brother's heart.

"She died," she says, softly, and I feel like someone's knocked all the air out of me. "She got sick. Started getting some cramps and twinges in her legs, at first. Dropping things. She eventually went to the doctor, but there was nothing they could do. Some sort of motor neuron disease. I forget the name of it, but it progressed way faster than even the doctors were expecting.

"Of course, Aiden insisted on caring for her, and she insisted he not burden himself with it. She stopped him from visiting the hospital in the end, when she was so sick she couldn't bear being seen. So security would come and take him away every time he tried to get in. It just completely devastated him."

Lexi's eyes look watery and haunted with the memory of it. I can feel a huge, gnawing grief in the pit of my stomach at the thought of how bad that time must have been for Aiden. And for Sophie. I can barely imagine how it must have been for Lexi, watching her brother go through that.

"He was in no state to study after she died," she says. "Took a year out and spent it up at the resort with Dave, helping out. He taught people to ski and did odd jobs around the place. Dave said he barely stopped from dawn 'til dusk, just threw himself right into it so he could block it out all day, and then be too exhausted at night to do anything but sleep when he was alone with his thoughts."

"Jesus," I breathe.

"Yep," says Lexi, sniffing. She composes herself a little. "Anyway, he went back to college after that year, but just threw himself right into it the same way. Then threw himself into work when he graduated. It's like he's been running away from the possibility that anything like that would ever happen to him again. And then he met you," she says, smiling at me.

I smile back at her, but I feel the smile contort on my face. "Oh, God," I say. I press my hands to my face. "And I had my stupid rules because of a petty breakup with a nobody."

"No, no. You can't blame yourself, Pippa," she says. "He knew your rules, and he agreed to them. But as soon as you were gone he knew he'd made a mistake. So he threw himself back into work again."

"Wow," I say.

"Yes, but like I said earlier—I believe in fate. And if that whole situation hadn't played out the way it did back in March, he probably wouldn't have gone at it quite so hard with work. And if he hadn't, then he wouldn't have ended up moving here. So you see?" she says, reaching over and placing her hand on my arm, kindly. "The universe has a way of working itself out."

"Yeah," I agree, though I feel a little guilty for being more open with Lexi about my feelings for her brother than I've ever been with him.

"Hey, Lexi," I say, finally putting the sandwich back down on the arm of the chair. There are bits of bread glued to my fingers, and I have to wipe my hands in my coveralls again before I reach for a pen and paper. "Will you do me a favor and pass a note onto Aiden?"

"Of course," she says, smiling. "If you'll do me a favour and not mention that I told you all this. I feel like it's his place to tell you in his own time. Maybe he never will. But I think it's important for you to know."

My pen pauses on the paper. I try to try to get rid of the protest that's wriggling and writhing behind my sternum. I start jotting down my number, but the nagging feeling won't give in. It bubbles up into my throat, and I know I'm not going to be able to pretend. Steeling myself, I look up at her.

"Lexi, look. I... you've been so kind to me and so cool, offering me the profile and all. But I can't make that promise to you. I really, really like your brother. I don't want to lie to him, you know? Or pretend that I don't know about something this important."

To my surprise, Lexi nods and sighs, taking the note from my hand and folding it up to place into her purse. "Alright. I can respect that. And I guess I'm pleased you're serious about him. No that I doubted it, but... you know. I don't think he really knows how to do casual. I'll tell him I told you."

I nod, gratefully.

"So I haven't actually confirmed with him that I'll be there on Christmas day," I say.

"But you will be, right?" Lexi asks. "Did your roomie say yes?"

"Yes," I nod. Valerie had said yes almost before I finished asking her. She's been dying to meet Aiden ever since she found out he moved here and I've been seeing him again. "So just let us know what time to—"

I cut off as a tight, sharp pain closes around my abdomen and takes my breath away. Wincing, I place my hand on my side and bend forward, shifting in the chair. There's a flash of nausea, and little stars bloom in my peripheral vision.

Lexi is immediately alert, sitting up straight and reaching out her hand to my shoulder. "Are you alright?" she asks, her face awash with concern.

The pain lingers around, strange and surreal and unexpected, before it disappears just as quickly as it came, fading away to nothing in a moment. I manage to nod to Lexi.

"I think I might be gluten intolerant or something," I say, looking up at her face. Her expression is skeptical, but I can't think of any other reason for it. I manage a weak smile. "It's been happening a bit lately. I'll get tested after the holidays. I'm sure it's just the universe telling me to eat more salads."

Now that the pain has eased completely, and I've managed to fix my smile, Lexi looks a bit more willing to let it go. I can't say I'm not worried, but I really can't afford to be sitting around in doctors' offices while this deadline is looming and my studio is on the line.

"I'll make us a drink," says Lexi, getting up and moving to the makeshift little kitchen in the corner of the studio. It's really not much, but there's a small kettle, a counter-top fridge that occasionally rattles, and enough breakfast tea and coffee to keep the rare visitors happy.

"I'm not going anywhere until I know you're alright," she says. "Coffee? Or tea?"

She reminds me so much of Aiden with her sudden need to care for me and make sure I'm alright, I almost laugh. I ask for coffee, and for the next hour we sit and chat, about the magazine feature, about the bastard who now owns the studio, about Christmas and gifts and life in general. She cancels two meetings while we're sitting there, chatting and laughing, but she finally decides I'm alright when I've made it through three cups of decaf pain free, and she gets up to leave.

"See you Christmas Day, then," she says, as she hugs me.

"And don't let Aiden choose a sickly looking, wonky tree. Promise me."

I promise, laughing, and wave goodbye to the second Coleman I've watched leave in a chauffeur-driven car this week.

AIDEN

Christmas Eve, 2018

As soon as Lexi gave me that little piece of paper with Pippa's number written on it, I sent a text. We've been texting off and on since then, but not nearly enough for my liking. I have meetings; she has her deadlines. I don't want us to be in each other's business all day every day, but it's been over a week since I saw her, now. I'm forgetting the softness of her lips and the scent of her hair, and I'm not happy about it. So it's with no lack of excitement that I half-skip out to the car and greet Dev on the morning of Christmas Eve.

"Morning, Dev! We're heading to get Pippa."

"Aha! I thought you looked happier than I've seen you all week," Dev replies, grinning broadly.

We get to Pippa's street just before noon, and I send her a text to let her know we've arrived. I get out of the car myself to wait for her to come down, stomping around in the snow to keep warm and occasionally blowing into my hands.

"Hey!" she calls from behind me. I spin around to see her grinning, skipping down the steps and blowing plumes of steamy breath into the icy cold air.

"Hey, sexy," I say, wrapping my arms around her as she gets close enough. I lean down and kiss her, desperately, deeply, trying to compensate for every second we've been apart. I feel her small hands grip at the front of my coat as she leans up on the tips of her toes, kissing me back just as eagerly. When she pulls away, she's grinning from ear to ear.

"Miss me?" she asks. I don't answer. Instead, I pull her in and kiss her again, deeper, and longer.

"I guess so, huh?" she says.

"I'll never tell!" I grin. "Let's find a Christmas tree."

We head for the car, hand in hand. Dev is standing beside the door, stoic and professional, and he opens it for us to get in.

The ride to the Christmas tree farm doesn't take long, once we're free of the outer city traffic, and the ride is mostly along rural roads where the scenery sprawls out on either side like a winter wonderland. I tuck Pippa in under my arm, and enjoy the feeling of having her there, and the relief that things feel as natural as they ever have.

I was a bit concerned, after Lexi told me that she'd told Pippa about Sophie, that things might be a bit awkward. After I chewed Lexi out—and then apologized for having done so—I managed to compose myself a bit and reason that Pippa really isn't the type to compare herself to a dead girl, or to be jealous or uncomfortable about something like that. I guess that's why I'm able to think about the fact that I'm falling in love with her—even if I can't bring myself to speak about it out loud, yet, to the person who deserves to hear it most.

We pull into the farm and get out, and we're greeted by a middle-aged, rugged-faced lady who emerges from a small, fairy-lit cabin and shakes our hands enthusiastically with a big, broad smile. The happy little melody of *Frosty the Snowman* floats out of the open cabin door behind her.

"Heeey!" she says, "I'm Sara, and I own the place. Let's get you two lovebirds a tree, shall we? First Christmas together? I can smell new love, me. Lovely thing, it is. Now, follow me."

Having been introduced to Sara without playing any role in the conversation whatsoever, we begin to traipse through the snow behind her. Pippa and I look at each other, and I can tell she's struggling as much as I am not to laugh.

"Now then," says Sara, after we've walked a good ways along a huge field, and past hundreds and hundreds of big, bushy Christmas trees. "Take your pick down there," she says, pointing down one row of trees. "Any one you like. It's a great batch this year."

I can hear wheels on gravel in the distance, and it seems to be Sara's cue to go off and give herself another welcome chat.

"Give me a shout when you've picked one out and I'll get one of the guys to come and chop for you," she calls. "Enjoy!"

And just like that, Pippa and I are left alone.

"I like the green ones," she says, and I snort a laugh.

"Well I like the ones made of wood, so how are we going to choose?"

We stroll down the row a little way, looking up and down the trees that are all standing there, waiting to be picked. I stop near a sickly looking, bent little tree and tilt my head. I can't help it. Lexi always hates the trees I pick out, but there's something about having all this choice and picking the most scrawny, pine-bare tree that tickles me.

SPLAT.

I feel it hit square between my shoulder blades and straighten. I know exactly what it is before I turn around and see Pippa standing there, laughing, packing together a second snowball with her gloved hands.

"Step away from the scrawny tree!" she says, holding the

snowball up in one hand, ready to launch. "Strict orders from Lexi. Hands up!"

She's enjoying this way too much.

"Stop," I say, putting my hands up. "Don't shoot!"

A peal of joyful laughter hits me just a split-second before the second snowball does.

"You little—" I say, leaning down to grab a handful of snow. I hear her squeal and look up to see her running away. I launch and miss, my snowball crumbling against a large tree trunk.

"Come back here!" I call, following the sound of her laughter.

I round a tree that sounds like it's giggling, and the first hint I get that she's waiting for me is a snowball smacking me on the side of my head. Little bits of snow cling to my hair and start to melt, dripping down the side of my face.

"You're in for it, Pip!" I call. I bend down to add a bit more snow to my snowball, and stalk after her, entirely focused on payback.

I can't hear her laughing any more, and when I step out into the space between two rows of trees, I can see why.

She's on the floor on one knee, doubled over, holding her stomach.

"Pippa!" I call, tossing my snowball aside. "What is it? What's wrong?"

I get down beside her, my hand on her back, leaning down to search her face. She's pale as can be and her whole face is screwed up with pain.

"What happened?"

She groans and takes a deep breath.

"Stomach pain," she says, through gritted teeth. "It'll be alright in a minute."

Every synapse in my body fires at once. Concern and fear and anger flood through me. "It'll be alright" are the very same words I heard from Sophie, time after time after time, before she finally went to see a doctor.

"We're going to a doctor," I tell Pippa. There's that edge to my voice again, but I don't care. I need her to look after herself. I need to look after her. And I'm not going to take no for an answer.

To my surprise, she doesn't argue with me. She blows out a steady breath from pursed lips, and nods. I help her to her feet and hold out my arm, which she takes without thinking about it.

I slow my stride and take my time, making sure she can easily keep up without straining herself, and we walk slowly back toward the car, along the rows and rows of trees.

"Nothin' you fancied?" says Sara as we pass. I shake my head to her and wave, not lingering to explain.

We're almost back at the car. Dev sees us coming and gets out, opening the back door for us. Just as he looks over, I hear a gasp and I feel Pippa go down again beside me, her grip on my arm tightening as she tries to stay on her feet. In my peripheral vision, I see Dev start quickly toward us, and I turn into Pippa, letting her grab around my neck to hold herself up. She's whimpering and panting, and I feel utterly, utterly helpless.

"What's wrong?" says Dev, arriving beside us.

"I don't know," I tell him, leaning down to lift Pippa into my arms and carry her the rest of the way. "But we're going to the emergency room."

She doesn't protest about me carrying her. She looks completely miserable, now, her face contorted with pain I don't know how to ease. Dev runs on ahead to open the car, and together, the three of us manage to get Pippa into the back seat.

It's the longest ride of my life, and Pippa cries out in pain every few minutes. I don't know how to help her, so I just hold her gently, trying not to make things worse, and feeling impotent as I shush pathetic, soothing sounds at her, and tell her we'll be there soon.

Dev pulls into the emergency bay, and we both help Pippa into the hospital. As the slightly stale, medicinal smell of the place hits me, a thousand old unwanted memories come flooding back, and it's all I can do to keep myself from being overwhelmed by them.

Not again. Please, not again.

"WE NEED A DOCTOR!" I scream, wildly, as we round the corner to the reception desk.

PIPPA

We've been here for an hour and I haven't seen a doctor yet. I'm sick of nurses asking me questions about my medical history and admin staff asking me questions about my insurance and address, and I'm sick of this stupid pain that keeps coming in waves, hitting me like a truck every time and then fading away to leave me feeling exhausted and scared. Thank god for Aiden. And Dev.

Dev has texted Valerie for me, since my phone is in some lockbox somewhere with the rest of my stuff, and Aiden hasn't left my side since we got here. He's answered every question he can on my behalf, and poured me water from the dispenser a couple of times, insisting I drink.

"You're…" says one nurse, who seems particularly put out that this hot adonis is here, answering all the questions she asks me.

"Her boyfriend," he says, and despite the waves of pain and the fear I'm feeling, I get a little thrill out of that.

"My boyfriend, huh?" I ask, when she's gone.

"You're goddamn right," he says, nodding. He looks at me. I know I'm a mess. My hair is stuck to my forehead, my clothing has been pulled and prodded by all the nurses in turn, and I'm pale as a ghost. But so is he. He looks tense from the top of his head to the tips of his toes, and I guess that it has something to do with Sophie.

"Gosh, how romantic," I tease, trying to make him feel a little better.

It must work, because he shakes his head at me and leans in, using his fingers to un-stick the hair from my face. "I think it's your ability to be sarcastic in even the most dire circumstances that I like about you most," he says, and I grin.

"Okay, boyfriend."

The curtains flash open, and Valerie bursts in through them.

"Pip!" she shouts, heading right over and throwing her arms around me. Aiden just about manages to get out of the way.

"Oh my god, are you alright? What's wrong? What happened? What can I do?" she asks, rapid-firing questions at me. "I ditched the office as soon as I got the message."

"It's alright," I say, and she finally stops squeezing me, but she stays bent over me, her hands on my upper arms. "I've just been having some stomach pains. The nurse told me the doctor will be in shortly."

"Valerie?"

Aiden's voice makes both of us turn toward him. He's staring at Valerie with a look of utter confusion, that she returns as soon as she sees him. There's a long moment of silence, where the only sound is the distant beeping of medical monitors and the bustle of the emergency room just beyond the curtains.

Valerie looks at me, then back at Aiden.

Aiden looks at me, then back at Valerie.

"Oh my God," they say in unison. They each lift their hands and extend a forefinger to point at each other. "You're…"

It's like something out of a comedy movie, and I'm just sitting here, watching the surreal scene play out before me.

"Oh, my God!" says Valerie again. She laughs and slaps her hand to her forehead. "Of course. Aiden. Moved to NYC. Lawyer. I can't believe I didn't put it together."

"Uhh... hello?" I say, looking from one to the other of them, still clueless.

"He's my boss!" Valerie says, with disbelief written all over her face. "You're dating my boss, Pip."

Aiden's face splits into a wide grin and he laughs, too. I'm just about to burst into laughter when another pain hits me right in the gut. It feels like something is squeezing right around my middle, digging knives into me at the same time.

They're both on edge immediately.

"Okay, it's a joke that a doctor hasn't been in here yet," I hear Aiden say, before he disappears out of the cubicle. Valerie rubs my back while I cringe my way through the wave of pain, and just as I'm recovering, Aiden returns with a doctor in tow. By the look on her face, Aiden has been... firm, in his request that I be seen.

"Alright," says the doctor. "If you two can step out to the waiting room while I examine Ms. Long, I'll have someone fetch you when we're done here."

Neither of them look eager to leave, but I assure them it's fine and they both go out. I can hear their fading conversation as they go, talking about how small a world it is.

"Alright," says the doctor, again, pulling on a pair of gloves. "Now, Phillippa. I'm Dr. Sarah James. Sarah is fine. Abdominal pain can be a tricky symptom to get to the bottom of. I'm just going to have a feel around and see if we can find any particularly tender spots. I need you to tell me if anything gives you undue pain. Especially if it's a similar pain to the one you've been experiencing, alright? If you could just lay down and lift your top for me, please."

I nod and lay down, pulling my top up to just under my

bra, and my pants down to just below my tummy. She begins feeling around, first just beneath my ribs on one side, then the other, and then a little lower. I feel her hands pause and watch her face change to a small frown. Her fingers move again, a little lower. She presses, pauses, then look up to my face.

"Just a moment, Phillippa," she says, and slips out of the curtains. She returns a moment later with a trolley that has a screen and a keyboard, and a long, coiled wire attached to some sort of wand.

"Just a little cold and wet now, Phillippa," she says, and squirts some sort of gel onto my stomach.

"Pippa," I say, a little annoyed at the repeated use of my full name. I usually only hear that when my mother is disappointed about something I've done, and being annoyed at least half-distracts me from the rising panic I can feel behind my sternum as I realize that it's an ultrasound machine. She keeps the screen facing away from me, and I manage to convince myself that she's found some sort of huge tumour that's about to do me in.

"Mmm," the doctor says, pressing the wand around on different parts of my abdomen. "Okay. I just want a second opinion, Pippa," she says, and I stare at her and numbly nod. I wish Aiden or Valerie were here.

Again she leaves the cubicle, and again she returns, this time with another doctor in tow—a man in scrubs who looks harried and tired.

"Just here," says Dr. James, pressing the wand thing against my stomach again. The other doctor doesn't even look at me. He looks at the screen and tilts his head one way, then the other as the wand moves about and cold jelly is spread all over my abdomen.

"Mmm," he says, much the same way Dr. James did a moment ago. "Yes, definitely."

"Thank you," says Dr. James, and the other doctor leaves the room.

"Is it bad news?" I ask.

"Well," she answers, and I can tell she's trying to be gentle and diplomatic. "I suppose that depends on you, really. You can clean up. Thank you."

"What do you mean?" I ask, taking the paper towel from her and wiping the residual gel from my tummy.

"Well, there's no way to break this to you gently, Pippa," she says, waiting for me to rearrange my clothing. She sits on the edge of the bed and places her hand on my arm. My heart is thundering in my chest all of a sudden. This is the sort of bedside manner that's rehearsed at med school for a terminal diagnosis, surely.

"It looks like you're in labor." Her words sound soggy, like I'm hearing them through a soaked sponge.

"What?" I snort the word out, half-laughing.

"There is a fully grown baby in your abdomen and it looks like it's coming out very soon," she says, in a measured, plain tone. "I can't be certain that you're in active labor right now, but you're definitely near term, so we'll get you down to the maternit—"

"No there's not," I tell her, sitting bolt upright. She looks at me with a neutral expression, as though she's waiting for me to go on. I don't disappoint. "There is not a baby in my abdomen!" I insist. "There can't be. How can there be? I haven't even had sex since…"

"About nine months ago?" she offers.

I feel like the entire world has just crashed down on me. Like every atom in the known universe is suddenly putting pressure on my body from every angle, all at once. March. Nine months ago it was March. And I was on a ski holiday. With Aiden.

"But I've been getting periods," I tell her.

"Pippa," she says, patiently. "Some women get what seem

like periods when they're pregnant, some women get no morning sickness or other signs of pregnancy. It's very rare that this happens, but I can assure you that it does, and that it's happening to you. I know it's a lot to take in, but you may be giving birth in a matter of hours, and you need to be ready for it. Will I tell your friends for you?" she asks.

I don't know what the hell to say to that. I'm trying to comprehend the fact that I'm in labor. With a human baby. Inside me. I haven't even begun to wrap my head around it yet. So I just nod, mutely, and sit there as she leaves the cubicle, trying to absorb the shock wave from the bombshell that's just been dropped into my life.

AIDEN

Valerie and I are still laughing about how unlikely our little triangle is, when the doctor pops her head into the waiting room. Catching my eye, she beckons me over. Valerie and I stand up together and walk a little ways down the corridor with the doctor before she guides us into a family room.

I've been in this sort of room before. With Sophie. I know the sort of news that's broken in these rooms. My heart is suddenly thrumming away, beating so hard I feel like I might keel over. My legs all but give way and I almost collapse into one of the seats.

"Is she alright?" asks Valerie, and I'm suddenly grateful that she's there to do the talking. I'm not certain my voice would work if I tried to talk right now. My tongue feels dry and rough, and I'm acutely, strangely aware of it taking up too much room in my mouth.

"Yes. She's a little shocked, but she's alright," says the doctor. Valerie and I exchange glances.

"Shocked at what?" says Valerie.

"Well. We did some investigation, and it turns out that she may be in labor," says the doctor. Just like that.

At first, I assume that this must be some strange figure of speech, or maybe a joke. There's silence while Valerie and I stare at the doctor.

"In... labor? Like... a baby?" says Valerie, mouth agape.

"Yes. Like a baby," nods the doctor. "Exactly."

"Oh my God," Valerie says, quietly.

I suddenly find myself on my feet - I don't know how, or why. I'm just aware of the blood rushing to my head in an effort to catch up with it. The doctor gets to her feet, too, and Valerie follows.

"We're not certain that she's in active labor right now. We'll have her transferred to the maternity unit and they'll take it from here."

"Woah. Woah, woah. Woah." I can hear my own voice, but it feels so distant. I'm shaking my head and holding my hands up to the doctor to try to stop her talking. I just need a minute to breathe. A minute to understand. "Pippa's having a baby?"

"Yes. It's very unusual that a woman would be this far along without knowing, but it's not entirely unheard of. She's going to need a birthing partner."

"Shit," I hear myself say. My hand is raking through my hair and I'm pacing, and when I glance to Valerie she's looking me up and down.

"And a lot of moral support," the doctor goes on. "She's pretty shaken up. I can only let one of you in while we prep her for transfer, but once she's settled in at the maternity unit, you'll both be able to be with her until she moves to a birthing room. So which of you will go in?"

I see Valerie turn to look at me in my peripheral vision. When I look back at her, she's expectant, like she's waiting for me to offer. But I can't. I'm rooted to the spot, frozen in place. My mind can't comprehend what I've just heard and I can't figure out how the hell I fit into this picture. I want to jump to the rescue, rush to her side and be the hero, but my brain is overwhelmed with too many conflicting urges. The fear I felt when I saw Pippa doubled over like that in the snow. The memories of Sophie that have been dredged up by the clinical, chemical smells of the hospital. I can't think straight.

"Aiden?" Valerie says. I keep staring, silently, utterly dumbstruck.

"Jesus," Valerie says, and she makes the decision for me, shoving past me, shoulder first, and heading for the room that Pippa is in. I hear the doctor mutter something about taking all the time I need as she closes the door behind her.

I don't know how long I stand there for. At one point, I look down at my fingers and mutter "March, April, May," as I lift them, one by one. And then I stop. I already know it's my baby. I know it in my bones, with more certainty than I've ever known anything. And suddenly, through the fog of ancient anxiety and pain, through the beeps and whirrs of the hospital, through the cloying stench of the place, comes the urgent, sudden realisation that I need to be with her. Now. Forever. Always.

I dash out of the little family room and run along the corridor, almost knocking a nurse over on the way. It seems endless. The strip lights pass overhead, long streaks of clinical white, and I skid my way around the corner into the treatment area she was in, over to the cubicle, tearing back the curtain.

"Pippa, I—"

She's not there. Neither is Valerie.

The bed sheets are still messed up and there's a strange looking machine beside the bed that wasn't there before. Just as it sinks in that it's an ultrasound machine, one of the nurses who grilled Pippa earlier walks in.

"Where is she?" I demand, pointing my finger at the bed. "Where's Pippa?"

"Oh," says the nurse, so cheerily that I want to scream. I

must look like a lunatic, because she smoothes out her voice and speaks to me in a soothing tone. "Nothing to panic about. She's just being transferred. They left about... ooh. Ten minutes ago?"

Ten minutes? My heart lurches. *Shit.* How long was I standing in that room, wallowing? When I should have been here, with Pippa? This is terrifying for me; I can't begin to imagine what it's like for her.

"Where?" I ask, staring at the nurse, my voice urgent. It's a demand, not a request, and her benign smile is really starting to piss me off.

"Here," she says, walking around the bed. She takes me by the arm and guides me back to one of the endless, cold corridors. "Down there, take a right. All the way at the end of the corridor, you'll see the elevator. Up one floor, and when you get out, follow the signs. You can't miss them," she says. "The ones for the maternity unit are all multicolored."

"Down here," I repeat, to make sure I've got it. "Right. Elevator. One floor. Multicolored signs."

"That's right," she says, with a nod.

I'm already in the middle of my second long, half-run stride, when I hear the nurse again.

"Sir?"

I turn my head, still moving. The nurse is smiling at me. *Smiling.*

"Congratulations!" she says.

By the time I get to the elevator, I'm breathless. I stand there jabbing repeatedly at the button on the wall, cursing under my breath and drawing strange looks from the woman who's standing beside me, holding a blue, helium-filled balloon that reads "It's a boy!" in big, happy letters sprawled across the shiny foil.

It feels like it takes an eternity for the elevator to arrive, but when it does I step inside, turn around and glare at the woman, my finger on the hold button while I wait for her to get in. I realize I must look like a crazy person, so I try to force a friendly smile onto my face. It does not seem to help.

"I'll get the next one," she says, waving her hand for me to go on ahead. I jab at the button to take me up one floor and pace around the elevator like a caged animal. It only takes about twenty seconds, but when seconds are passing like hours, it feels like a lifetime.

The nurse wasn't wrong about the signs. I notice the first one immediately when the elevator doors open. It's bright red and blue and yellow, and there are little balloons and teddy bears dotted around it. The big arrow points to my right, so I turn that way and speed down the corridor. Another two turns and I see the same color scheme on a big, curved sign above double doors that reads "MATERNITY UNIT".

I don't even notice the desk beside the unit entrance until I slam shoulder-first into the unyielding doors and bounce back off them.

"Shit," I hiss, and take a step back, looking around frantically for some kind of button or intercom. Anything that will let me get inside.

"Excuse *me*," says a voice, sharply.

I turn to my right and spot the desk, and the pointy-featured, too-thin woman who stands behind it, hands placed firmly on her hips, looking at me over the type of half-moon eyeglasses I didn't even know existed anymore. The thin lines all around her lips look like they could only have been achieved through a lifetime of scowling.

"I need to get in," I blurt.

"Well, that may be so," she says, looking me up and down. I can already tell she's going to be trouble, and I can feel a rage starting to build in the pit of my stomach. "But we can't just let any old Tom, Dick or Harry into the birthing rooms, can we? What's the name of the patient?"

"Pippa," I say, trying to get a hold of myself. "Uh. Phillippa Long."

The receptionist looks down at the screen in front of her, bends a little, and starts two-finger clacking something into the keyboard.

"Please," I say. I can hear the desperation in my voice, but the crone behind the desk is unmoved.

"A *moment*," she says, irritably. Clack...... clack.

It takes all the restraint I have to stand there, attempting to look patient while she tries to get her bony old fingers to work the keyboard. I grind my teeth and take a couple of long breaths, but nothing dampens the rising irritation. I'm transported back to the hospice that Sophie was in towards the end, standing at the door, begging them to let me in while doctors and nurses, Sophie's parents, and eventually the cops, drag me away time after time after time. I can feel rising anger, now, roiling behind my sternum.

""She already has someone with her," the receptionist says, eventually.

"Yes, I know," I say, "bu—"

"But nothing," she says, pointedly. "Only one visitor until after assessment."

"Right, but I need t—"

"Sir," she says, with the practiced prickliness of a school marm. This woman might as well be a porcupine. "I understand that you're frust—"

"Jesus CHRIST!" I shout, slamming my hand down on the counter as my barriers collapse and all the rage and anxiety comes flooding out. I see her start and reach down beneath the desk, but I've already dealt with my fair share of obstinate, obstructive hospital staff in my lifetime, and right now, right here, I can't deal with it any more.

"*Please* open the door," I say, much more aggressively than is productive.

"Sir, I need you to calm down," she says, her expression impassive.

"*I AM CALM!*" I yell.

Two security guards appear around the corner, and I guess it's my less-than-convincing assertion that I'm calm that persuades them to immediately restrain me. I shrug away from the first hand that tries to grab my upper arm.

"You're leaving," says the bigger one of them. He's the same height as me, pudgy around the middle. I could probably take them both if I was quick enough. But the door would still be locked and the bony old gatekeeper would probably call the cops.

"With us or with the cops," says the smaller of the two, confirming my fear. They close in and try to take my arms again, but I shrug them off.

"Alright," I say. "Alright. I'm leaving."

I don't know how I manage to persuade myself to go quietly, instead of doing something stupid; nor how I manage to convince myself not to cuss out the crone behind the desk as she stands there looking smug, watching me leave with her arms folded over her chest; but before I know it, I'm outside in the snow, blowing clouds of cold air and looking back at the hospital entrance while the guards stare me down.

I'm banned from the hospital premises for twenty-four hours, they tell me. If I try to re-enter, they'll call the cops and I'll be arrested and spend a night in jail.

Perfect.

"Just fucking perfect," I mutter as I stalk back to the car. Dev sees me coming and gets out to open the door.

"How is she?" he asks, concern on his face.

"Not now, Dev," I say, shaking my head. I've never felt so dejected in my life, and I just can't bear having to explain.

"Yes, Boss," says Dev, dutifully. "Home?"

"Home," I confirm, getting into the back of the car.

Dev closes the door, and I flick a switch to turn off the intercom, and another to black out the glass between the front and back of the car. I'm despondent and dejected. If I'd only been a little faster. If I'd only put my own hatred of hospitals, my ancient anxieties and my shock aside to be there for Pippa, none of this would have happened.

Pippa. What the hell is she going to think of me? I close my eyes and cringe at the thought. The first time she's ever really needed me and I've failed. And now, with the threat of cops and a night in jail to keep me in check, there's nothing I can do about it.

As I stare out of the window, it begins to snow heavily. The cars slow down, and a thick blanket of fresh flakes begins to cover old footprints and tyre marks. I remember Pippa's beaming, dimpled face as she stood outside the coffee house, her hand held up with that perfect, unique little snowflake sitting on the end of her finger. I'd give anything to see that dimple again, right now.

PIPPA

Tick... Tock...

I've never known a clock to be quite so infuriatingly loud as the one on the back wall of the hospital cubicle. Nor as infuriatingly slow. I sit there, in the cubicle, staring at a crease in the curtain and trying to come to terms with the news I've been given.

There is a baby inside me. A fully grown baby that's ready, or nearly ready, to come out. How exactly *does* someone come to terms with finding out like this? Most people get months to reconcile themselves with an unplanned pregnancy. I get hours. And then there's the fact that it's Aiden's, that we've only just met again after months, and the baby was conceived during what was supposed to have been a week-long fling. And I love him. I think.

"Crazy," I whisper.

While I'm still alone, waiting for Valerie to return and wondering if Aiden will, I take the opportunity to look down at my tummy. It doesn't look much different than it ever has. There's a bit more protrusion than there used to be, but I assumed that was just an effect of me losing a few pounds.

Tentatively, slowly, I bring my hands up and place them over my tummy.

I could have done this exact thing yesterday, even this morning, and felt nothing. Now, there's a strange emotion attached to it as the knowledge that I'm pregnant begins to take root. My son or daughter is in there, hiding somewhere among all my insides, and in a very short while I'm going to meet them.

"Phillippa Long?"

I drop my hands quickly from my belly down onto the bed at my sides and snap my head up. A friendly looking woman in her forties has poked her head through the curtain. She's holding a clipboard and looking at me expectantly.

"Yes?" I say, half a question.

"Ah, good, good. I'm Amanda Andrews," she says, slipping quickly into the cubicle and extending her hand to me. "One of the counsellors here at the hospital."

I shake her hand and watch her warily, wondering what she's doing here.

"I'm just here," she says, taking a seat beside my bed, "to introduce myself and make sure I have your details correct, for now. I'll join you in the maternity unit when you're settled in there, and we can talk more."

The way she says it makes me feel like I'm going to be spending the rest of my life in the maternity unit.

"But if there's anything you want to ask me right now, go ahead and I'll do my best to answer."

"Do you have kids?" I ask her. I don't even know where the question comes from, but it pops out of my mouth before I even know I've thought it.

"I have four," she says, nodding and smiling.

Now that I have an answer, I don't know what to do with it. I nod at her and glance away, back to the crease in the curtain. I notice that it's changed shape a little, since

112

Amanda disturbed it on her way into my surreal little world.

"What's happening to you is very unusual, though," she says. "It's called cryptic pregnancy, and you're only the fifth I've seen in over twenty years in practice."

I look back to her and nod. She gives me another smile, this one more gentle, and her voice is a little quieter when she speaks again.

"Most of them involve an element of mental health issues, or abuse," she says.

It dawns on me that she's asking a question, and my brows lift.

"Oh!" I say, shaking my head. "Oh, no. Nothing like that. I just had a vacation fling and... but... I was on the pill. And we used condoms. I didn't even suspect..."

She nods. "And then you had a pregnancy that didn't give you any hint of its presence," she says. "Phillippa—"

"Pippa," I say.

"Sorry. Pippa" she says, jotting it down quickly on her notepad. "Whatever you're feeling at the moment—shock, surprise, fear... even disgust—it's all perfectly normal."

I know that she means well, and I understand what her job is here, but I'm just not ready to open up to a stranger right now. The clock tick-tocks away behind me, and I find myself wondering where Valerie is. Where Aiden is. How they're taking the news.

Amanda seems to take a hint I didn't realize I was giving. After promising that we'll talk more later, she starts reeling through my particulars so that I can confirm for the eighth time today that they're right.

"Pip!"

Valerie is back in an instant, and I physically sigh with relief to see her. Amanda makes her excuses and leaves, and Valerie sits on the bed with me, holding my hand.

"Wow," she says, looking at me. She's not smiling and

trying to make light of the situation, but she's not looking like she's at a funeral, either. "A baby, huh?"

I smile weakly and glance at the curtain behind her.

"Yeah," I reply, half-distracted. Maybe he's outside making a call. Or maybe he's in a cab on his way to the airport to catch a one-way flight to Timbuktu.

"I'm pretty terrified, Val," I admit. "I don't even know how it's possible to be about to give birth and not know you're pregnant. This is the sort of shit you see on reality shows that makes you think they're all made up."

"Not gonna lie," she says. "It's a bit crazy. But you'll deal. You always deal. And I'm here for you all the way."

I finally bite the bullet, swallow hard, and after another glance at the curtain, ask: "Aiden?"

I know her too well for her to hide her feelings from me. Maybe nobody else in the world would spot the minute twitch of her right eye that gives away her anger, but I see it straight away, standing out so much it might as well be a giant red flag waving in my face.

I screw my eyes closed tight. Valerie's arms are around me immediately, but they're wrong. The wrong arms. The right arms are attached to a man who is God-knows-where. And who could blame him?

I let her hold me for a while, and I cling to her while I try to stop myself bawling and attempt to realign my thoughts, away from Aiden's absence and back to what's going on right here, right now. I need to be preparing myself mentally for whatever is ahead of me. But as hard as I try, Aiden is all I can think about.

"What did he say?" I ask, when I feel like I can talk without sobbing.

"Nothing," she says, immediately. I don't even need to wonder if she's telling the truth. She always has. "He looked shell-shocked. He stood there in the little room with the doctor, staring at the wall. Distant. She said one of us needed to come in, so when he wasn't moving I did. Sorry, Pip, I just couldn't bear the thought of you in here alone, after the doctor told us what had happened."

"Aiden obviously could, though," I say, bitterly.

"You can't worry about that right now," she says. "You've got other things to think about. And for all you know, he's outside, waiting to get in. The doctor said only one of us could come in. He's probably just gone to get a coffee or something."

"Yeah," I say. I'm not convinced, but there's definitely a part of me that refuses to believe he'd leave me here, alone, about to have his baby. Unless he thinks it's not his baby. Or I've really misjudged him.

"Can I borrow your phone to text him, just in case?" I ask. "They've taken my stuff to the maternity unit."

"Out of battery," she says, with an apologetic look. "Sorry, Pips. I'll go find your phone as soon as we get to the other ward, alright?"

I nod, sighing.

The curtains open again and I look up eagerly, only to have my hopes dashed when a hospital porter enters, pushing a wheelchair.

"Phillippa Long?" he asks.

"Pippa," Valerie and I say together.

"Pippa," says the porter with a nod, and he pushes the wheelchair out a little, toward me. "Your chariot awaits."

I get down cautiously from the bed while Val gathers the magazines and unconsumed food from the bedside table, and we make our way to the maternity unit.

AIDEN

W hen I walk into my apartment, Dave has arrived. He and Lexi are decorating a Christmas tree in the corner. *Winter Wonderland* is playing quietly in the background, there's an open bottle of wine on the coffee table and a couple of half-drunk glasses beside it. Dave is standing with his arms stretched out either side of him and a tangled mess of tree lights connecting them, and Lexi is threading strings through baubles, ready to hang them. When she sees me, she gets to her feet and walks over.

"How is she?" she asks.

I know I'm white as a sheet. If I look even half as addled as I feel, then what Lexi's seeing is nothing good.

"Jesus, Aiden. What happened?"

"You got a tree," I say. I know it's the most ridiculous thing I could say, but how the hell do I find the words to explain everything to them? There's a baby on the way. And by baby on the way, I mean right now. I'm going to be a father. And I managed to get myself kicked out of the hospital and banned for 24 hours. Oh, and just in case you

116

needed a fairy on top, I doubt Pippa will ever want to see me again.

"Dev called and told us about Pippa being sick," says Dave, dropping the lights in a bundled mess on the floor. He walks over beside Lexi. "So we went and picked one up. Dude, what's wrong?"

I look up at him and manage a weak smile. I haven't seen him in months. He's grown a full beard and he looks good, apart from the frown of concern on his face.

"Uh," I say, reaching up and raking a hand through my hair. "She... uh. She's in labor," I blurt, finally.

They both freeze stock still, much like I did at the hospital, and I watch them both as the news seeps in and then realisation dawns on them. Dave's eyes narrow, and I already know that he's mentally counting the months since March.

"Then... why are you here?" says Lexi, eventually.

A glance at the half-decorated Christmas tree makes my top lip curl up in disgust. It should have been Pippa and I doing this. Standing here in this room, carefree, sipping wine and laughing and untangling Christmas lights.

"Because I'm a fucking idiot," I say, grabbing a bottle of whisky from the kitchen counter and pouring a large measure.

"Aiden... you didn't *leave* her there?" asks Lexi. I take some comfort from her disbelieving tone.

"Not by choice," I say, throwing the whisky down my throat and pouring more.

I don't look up. I already know what expressions they'll be wearing if I do. They'll have that half-concern, half-pity look that I haven't seen for years, and I can't bear to see it again. I'd rather stare into the bottom of my whisky glass. Just like last time.

"Mate," says Dave. "Tell us what happened."

I rub my face with my hands to try to push out some of

the pathetic self-pity and force myself to talk. I tell them about the farm, about her collapsing in pain.

"Oh!" Lexi interjects. "Something similar happened when I was with her at the studio. She doubled over with a sharp pain in her tummy."

"And you didn't mention it?" I say, looking at her aghast.

"No. Sorry." She frowns, regretfully. "I was so focused on the fact that I'd told her about Sophie. It slipped my mind."

I'd usually flinch at the mention of Sophie's name, or feel a wave of grief, or guilt. None of that happens this time. I'm laser-focused on Pippa, on our baby, on the fact that I'm not there.

I carry on, telling Dave and Lexi all about the hospital, the endless stream of nurses, the doctor. They're probably the only two people in the world who understand the way I feel in hospitals, so I tell them all of it. I tell them about Valerie, and that I froze, that I panicked, that by the time I got back to Pippa's cubicle she was gone. I tell them about the mad dash to the maternity unit, the crone at the reception desk, the security guards.

"Jesus," says Dave. I guess he instinctively understands how it must have felt for me, being refused entry. It was him who dealt with most of the fallout when I was turned away from visiting Sophie.

"At least she's not alone, anyway," says Lexi, and I have to admit that is a silver lining. Valerie might be mad at me right now, but I trust her, and there's some comfort in knowing that there's *someone* standing where I should be.

"So, they banned me for 24 hours," I tell them both. It seems like a good moment to throw back the second shot, so I do. The burn sinks down behind my sternum, and I welcome it like an old friend.

"So my baby is going to be born to the woman I've fallen head over heels in love with, and I'm not going to be there. I've tried her phone about thirty times, but it keeps ringing out. If she ever forgives me for this, it'll be a mira—"

"We'll see about that," says Lexi, interrupting me. She's suddenly striding across the room. She grabs her coat and Dave's from the stand beside the elevator, and throws Dave's to him. He just about catches it and turns to give me a questioning look.

"Lexi, they kicked me out," I say, shaking my head.

"And when did a little hurdle like that ever stop a Coleman?" she asks.

Bless this woman and praise whatever gods saw fit to make her my sister. I can feel a sudden bloom of hope rising up in me, a swelling warmth that pushes me to my feet and makes me believe, for just long enough, that I can salvage something out of this mess. And then, a sinking feeling.

"Dev will have taken the car home," I say.

"Dev doesn't have snow tyres, mate," says Dave, pulling his keys out of his pocket and jangling them in front of me.

I don't need any more persuading. I beat them both to the elevator, and inside a minute we're in Dave's truck.

The snow is really coming down, now. There are hardly any cars on the roads now, partly because it's late on Christmas Eve and partly because fat, fluffy snowflakes and white-out roads are making it difficult to see and difficult to drive. Dave is right at home, easily picking his way along the snow-laden roads while humming along to the Christmas tunes that float out of the radio.

I'm staring out of the window again, anxious, my leg bouncing up and down on the ball of my foot. I think back to the hospital, to the pain Pippa was in, to the way I felt when the doctor said she was having a baby. I keep coming back to one moment, though: when the nurse congratulated me.

"I'm going to be a father," I say out loud.

Lexi turns around in the front passenger seat and Dave looks at me in the rearview. They're both smiling.

"I love her, guys," I say.

"We know!" says Lexi.

"No shit!" says Dave, at the same time. "We've been waiting for you to catch up."

"Oh, hey! Dave, stop, man. Just for a minute."

He doesn't ask any questions. He pulls in at the side of the road and half-turns in his seat.

"Back in a minute," I say, and, leaving them both there looking perplexed, I head out into the snow and toward a department store that is, miraculously, still open.

There aren't many people left inside at this time, so I have the run of the place. I'm desperate to get to the hospital to see Pippa, so my shopping spree is a mad dash through the baby section and the ladies' clothing section, and a quick pit-stop at the jewelry counter, where I leave a very confused, very bewildered assistant in my wake. With a couple of grand rung up on my card, I head back out, put the packages in the trunk, and shove a giant teddy bear into the back seat of the truck before I get in behind it.

Lexi and Dave are looking at me as though my mind has finally snapped.

"What?" I ask, holding up my hands as if to plead my innocence. "Just a few necessities."

Once we're out of the city traffic, the run is smooth and fast. We soon arrive at the hospital and manage to find a parking space near the main entrance. From inside the car, Lexi nods toward it.

"Same guard?" she asks.

"Yeah. There were two of them earlier, though. I guess the other one's finished, or on a break or something."

"Okay, here's the plan," says Lexi, and starts to explain to Dave and I what's going to happen.

A few minutes later, Lexi is out of the car and sashaying through the snow, wearing her huge fake-fur coat and a pair of sunglasses that cover half her face. Dave and I have split off to opposite sides of the hospital, making our way stealthily through the car park so that the guard doesn't see us. I peek out from behind the corner nearest the entrance on my side, waiting for my cue. From my vantage point, the guard looks bored. That's a good sign.

"OH MY GOD!"

Dave's voice rings out, loud and unmistakable.

"Lexi! Lexi Coleman? Oh, man, I'm a HUGE fan!"

Around the corner, I have to bite my lip to stop myself from laughing. The plan is ridiculous, and something that only Lexi would've come up with - and it just might work. Even if it doesn't, the temporary reprieve from feeling on-edge is a relief.

Unable to resist, I peek out again. They've already caught the guard's attention. I can see him looking between Lexi and Dave, trying to fathom what's going on. He's probably trying to figure out who Lexi actually is and whether he recognizes her.

"HUGE fan!" says Dave, approaching Lexi from the other side of the doors. "Can I get an autograph?" he asks, and he gets right up close, inside her personal space.

Lexi, right on cue, takes a step back, looking uncomfortable and glancing to the security guard. I could probably get through the door without him noticing by now, but I decide to wait a bit longer to be on the safe side.

"Lexi, please?" says Dave, and grabs at the sleeve of her coat.

"UGH! Get away from me, creep!" Lexi says, feigning disgust and giving Dave a shove.

This is provocation enough for the guard—the bigger of the two from earlier—to step away from the door and head towards the pair of them, yelling: "Hey!"

I don't wait a second longer. As soon as he's away from the entrance, I slip inside and head quickly toward the maternity unit, following the same, brightly colored signs as earlier.

The closer I get to the unit and to Pippa, the faster my feet carry me. I ease up when I get to the corner just before the reception desk comes into view, and my heart skips a beat with pure joy when I realize there's been a shift change. Pinch-Face is nowhere to be seen. Instead, a plump and pleasant young nurse sits there, thumbing through her phone.

"Hey," I say. My heart is pounding now. Pippa is just beyond those doors.

"Hello," says the nurse, placing her phone down on the desk in front of her.

"I'm here to see Pippa Long," I say. I don't feel like I quite manage to hit the casual tone I'm going for, especially while the sound of my heart is hammering rhythmically in my ears, but the nurse doesn't seem to notice anything off.

"Long," she says, clacking away at the keyboard at break-neck speed.

"Ah," she says. "The doctor's just doing the rounds, but if you take a seat in the waiting area, I'll call you when you can go in."

It takes every shred of self-control I possess to smile and nod, and head for the waiting room just off the corridor. I can't risk being kicked out again. I can't risk squandering this chance to let Pippa know exactly how I feel.

Five minutes later, Lexi appears at the door.

"Hey," she says as she steps into the waiting room. Dave comes in after her, struggling to carry the huge teddy bear and several bags that I got from the department store.

"You shop like a woman," he says, dropping everything onto the floor in front of me.

"How did you get away?" I ask.

"Pretended it was a misunderstanding," says Lexi, pulling the ridiculous sunglasses from her face. "And then took him to one side to discuss an upcoming feature about blue-collar workers and their daily struggles, for which he would *of course* be a perfect fit, while Dave grabbed the stuff from the truck and snuck inside."

I laugh, impressed once again by her moxie. " Of course you did."

"Of course she did," says Dave.

"Well, we're in, aren't we?" says Lexi, smiling, and I have to concede that her plan worked perfectly.

Now that we're here, sitting in the waiting room, I keep feeling pangs of nervous energy splaying out through my chest. Lexi and Dave sit and chat, Dave teasing Lexi about her "pointless celebrity rag" and Lexi teasing Dave about being a neanderthal up on his snowy mountain. I keep slipping my hand into my pocket and fidgeting with the small box I got from the jewelry counter in the department store, and nervously glancing out of the door every time footsteps approach, only to be disappointed when it's just a random nurse or maintenance worker passing by.

"Taking their time, aren't they?" says Lexi, when we've been sitting there for ten minutes.

"Doctors' rounds," I say, clipped. "Don't even know what's happening." The tingling energy in my legs gets too much, and I stand up and start pacing.

"Aiden!"

I spin around at the sound of Valerie's voice, and she's standing in the doorway, staring at me. Or glaring. I can't tell which, right away, and I don't have enough mental energy set aside to think about it.

"Is she alright?" I ask.

Valerie nods, slowly, as her gaze passes to the other two, right over Dave and settling on Lexi. Her eyes go wide.

"Oh, wow," she says. "Lexi Coleman! I love your site—I've read you since you were just a blog."

Lexi beams at her, and I recall Pippa telling me that Valerie was a fan of Wirl. I only know Valerie as a consummate professional from work, so it's strange to see her standing there with a huge, fan-girl grin on her face. I take it as a good sign that Pippa is well, at least.

"Dave," says Dave, filling the silence. He leans forward to shake Valerie's hand.

"What's happening?" I ask. I know it comes out as a demand, and the look on Valerie's face is not appreciative, but my store of patience and moderation is running low. I see her gaze shift quickly to the huge teddy bear sitting in the corner of the waiting room, and the assortment of bags that have baby clothes and ladies' pajamas spilling out of them. Her expression softens a bit.

"She's alright. It's starting to sink in now. She was in labor, but it's stalled," says Valerie. Lexi, Dave and I all stare at her, silently listening. "There are no signs of distress, but the doctor says they're going to give her some medicine to get things moving again, since she seems to be full term and there are risks if they don't. I just came out to get a drink." She nods at the vending machine at the side of the waiting room. "She's been wondering where you've been," she says, deadpan. I can discern nothing from her tone.

"The doctor's gone now?" I ask, feeling my pulse pick up again.

As soon as she nods, I'm out of there. I grab the teddy and squeeze past her, out into the corridor, and run to the reception desk.

"Pippa Long?" I say to the nurse.

She looks up and smiles at me, her lips twitching amusedly at the teddy I'm carrying that's half my size. Her hand shifts and there's a low, sharp buzzing sound as the door unlocks. I feel like I've won some sort of tournament.

"Just at the end of the corridor," she says. "On the right."
I thank her, pull the door open, and step inside.

PIPPA

I've cried a few times, about Aiden not turning up, and flip-flopped between calling him every cuss word I can think of and trying to rationalize his absence, while Valerie has sat here with me, nodding and agreeing with whatever I say.

Now that she's gone to get some drinks, I'm left to sit quietly on the propped-up hospital bed and think. I think I've managed to come to terms with what's happening as best as I'll be able to before it actually happens, so instead of thinking about labor and pushing and all of that imminent drama, I find myself thinking about Aiden.

Things would be so much easier if he were here with me. I imagine him standing over my bed, like he was earlier, looking protective, getting irritated when the nurses keep pestering me with the same questions over and over. I close my eyes and lean my head back against the bed, thinking back to the cabin and the carriage ride around Central Park.

It's almost cruel, the way these most lovely memories are flooding into my mind, when he seems to have abandoned me in my hour of need. I feel a roll of anger bubbling up in my chest. I can even remember stupid, little things, like him placing his finger under my chin and telling me I'm beautiful, when I stood in the middle of a busy street in my work clothes, feeling anything but.

"Prick," I say, out loud.

"I know."

My eyes fly open and I sit bolt-upright in the bed.

Aiden is standing there holding a comically large teddy bear. To say he looks haggard would be an understatement. His hair is a mess, the bottoms of his jeans are damp and muddy, and he has a five-o'clock shadow under anxiety-riddled eyes.

"You left," I say quickly, frowning the accusation at him, and I'm mortified as, yet again, I feel tears spring up to my eyes and my bottom lip begins to quiver.

"Yes," he says, with real shame in his voice. "But not by choice. I got kicked out by security."

"What?"

"I'm sorry, Pip. I froze. When the doctor came out and told me about the baby," he glances down to my tummy, and I instinctively drop a hand onto it. "I just... it was shock. And hospitals," he says, glancing around the room. "God, I hate hospitals. I was so worried when you were in such pain. I felt like I was right back there with..."

"Sophie," I interject.

He nods, looking guilty, and despite the lingering anger, I want to reach out and hold him. But I don't. I'm not quite ready to forgive him yet.

"By the time I got a grip of myself and came in, they'd moved you down here. And then this goddamn harridan receptionist wouldn't let me in."

I press my lips together, restraining the urge to laugh as I imagine him being dressed down by the sour-faced old woman who was at the desk when I was brought in.

"She called security, and they kicked me out and banned me for 24 hours."

"But... you're here."

"Lexi and Dave pulled a stunt to get me in."

"Lexi and Dave are here?" I ask. Everything is beginning to slot into place in my mind.

"Yeah," he says, nodding. And then he shakes his head, looking a bit like a big, shaggy dog trying to shake off water. "Listen, Pip," he says, straightening. He drops the teddy onto a chair and steps over to the bed, sitting down on the edge of it. There is a tiny, reluctant part of me that wants to push him away, but as soon as he reaches for my hand and I feel his warm skin, familiar against mine, I look up to him.

"Listen," he says, looking deadly serious. "I love you."

My heart performs some sort of somersault in my chest, and I swallow hard, staring at him.

"I know it was only a week in the cabin, but it was the best week of my life... until I found you again. I'd been so convinced for so long that I'd just live out my days alone, half-empty, throwing myself into work like my life depended on it, to fill the void. And I know you're going through a lot right now, and this baby is a bigger shock to you than to anyone else, but, God, Pippa. I love you. I know it more clearly than I've ever known anything in my life.

"The world is turning upside-down, right now. For both of us. But the only thing I know for sure is that if I have to live upside-down, I want you right there with me, upside-down, too. And I know we didn't plan this..." he says, and places his hand down over mine, over my tummy, where our baby is nestled quietly, oblivious to all their parents' drama.

"But I want it. I want this Christmas to be the first of so, so many for us. And this doesn't change a thing," he says, glancing to my tummy.

I feel the first tear fall down my cheek, and Aiden uses his free hand to catch it before it reaches my chin, wiping it away.

"Well, alright," he goes on, with a little smirk on his mouth that pits his cheek with a dimple. "It's probably going to change quite a lot of things…"

A laugh bursts out of my mouth, and I feel a huge wave of relief. The tears are flowing freely down my cheeks, now.

"But it doesn't change the way I feel about you." He moves, getting up from the bed, and I feel my face pull into a puzzled little frown as I wipe the tears away with my hands.

"So. What do you say?"

He reaches into his pocket and pulls out a small box, turning it toward me. He opens it and drops down out of sight. I lean over a little to see him, down beside the bed… on one knee.

Realization starts to settle in and I gasp as I see the ring, holding a hand over my mouth in perhaps the most ridiculous, stereotypically girly reaction I've ever had to anything.

"Want to live upside-down with me, forever?" he asks, looking up.

Every emotion in the known universe seems to hit me at once. I feel almost light-headed with relief, and suddenly, without having to think about it, I know that I can face anything the world throws at me if I'm with Aiden. I don't trust myself to say anything without ugly-crying all over him —again—so I nod. I nod so much I feel like my head might fall off.

"Not bad, boss," I hear. I look up to see Valerie in the door, smiling, and Lexi and Dave crowding both her shoulders to see in. Dave is giving me a big thumbs up and grinning, and Lexi has tears in her eyes and gives me a happy little wave. Before I can return it, Aiden is on his feet with his arms around me.

He kisses me, and I melt into it, feeling all the pressure and worry and anxiety I've been feeling all day just melt right out of me. He cups my face in his hands, the ring box held awkwardly between his thumb and forefinger, and then pulls back to look at me.

"The ring definitely doesn't fit," he says, and I laugh as Valerie, Lexi and Dave crowd into the room. Aiden pushes the far-too-big ring onto my finger, and I'm suddenly receiving hugs and kisses from everywhere. I see Valerie hugging Aiden and Dave hugging the giant teddy bear, and Lexi is thumbing away on her phone to god-knows-who. I feel like a ton-weight has been lifted from my shoulders—so much so, that I've quite forgotten I'm in the middle of a stalled labor.

"Pippa," says the doctor I saw just a short while ago, walking back through the door. He stops dead, a clipboard in his hand, and his brows go up as his gaze flicks from Aiden to Dave and the teddy bear, to Valerie and then Lexi, who is now holding my hand and admiring the temporary ring as it dangles on my finger. The doctor smiles.

Everyone turns to look at him, and the room is suddenly silent.

"We have a birthing room available," he says, quietly. He's a small, neat man with an efficient air about him and an amiable smile. "Ready?"

My heart is hammering again, pounding away in my chest so hard I'm surprised I'm not being thrown around the bed. I swallow hard and shake my head. "Not really."

"You are," says Val, gently, leaning down to give me a hug. "You'll be great."

"Yeah," says Dave, putting the teddy back down on the chair. He comes over and gives me a hug, too. "And if you're not, Aiden will be right there with you for you to punch."

"Hey!" says Aiden. He looks a little tense again, but he's grinning. Dave pulls him into a bear hug with a lot of manly back-slapping, and I could swear that the big mountain-man is getting a little teary-eyed.

"We're not going anywhere, either," Lexi says, leaning down to kiss me on the cheek. "We'll see you soon."

"Alright, then," I say, and blow out a big sigh. I gather every ounce of inner strength I can muster and look up to the doctor. "Ready."

AIDEN

"HnngggyaaaAAAAAAH!"

What in the *ever-living fuck* possessed me to think this would be plain sailing?!? I think I was picturing a jaunt to the maternity unit, some clean little medical procedure, and then we'd head home with our baby in time to catch the evening news. I must have somehow, down the years, convinced myself that the movies exaggerate childbirth for the sake of drama. I was wrong. I was very, very wrong.

Pippa has been writhing in pain every few minutes since they injected her with something called Pitocin to "get things moving". Thinking back on the happy, reassuring smile on the doctor's face when he said those words, I am now convinced that he might actually be the world's most sadistic villain.

"HNGYAAAH!"

Pippa's nails dig into my arm as she dips her head and pants along with the nurse, waiting for the contraction to ease off. I've never felt so completely helpless as I do right now, standing beside her, rubbing my hand firmly across the lower back to try to ease the pain. We've been up and down in and out of the bed, into the shower, onto some huge beach-ball-looking thing, into a *pool* for God's sake, and now we're back here for the nurse to check how she's doing. The contractions are coming thick and fast, and this one hit just as Pippa lay back down.

"Okay, it's stopped," she says, breathing purposefully through pursed lips and nodding. She looks exhausted. Apart from screaming when the contractions peak, she's barely complained at all.

"Right, let's have a check," says the nurse, pulling on a pair of gloves and dipping down between Pippa's legs.

"Drink?" I ask, holding out a cup of water to her. The straw dangles about in front of her face. Pippa looks up at me and manages a wry little smile, shaking her head.

I can't blame her. I've probably offered her water a hundred times in the last hour, it being one of the only useful things I can actually do. I have an entire new vocabulary now than I did when I walked in. I now know *exactly* what a contraction is, I know that they have peaks, I know what crowning is, what dilation is and the numbers we're going for. The nurses are probably sick of answering my questions.

"Alright, we're at ten," says the nurse.

I didn't think it was possible for Pippa to squeeze my hand any harder, but she manages it.

"Ten centimeters?" I ask. The panic is probably writ large all over my face, and when I look down, I see the same thing on Pippa's.

I have to get a grip. I'm supposed to be here for her, supporting and helping her, not worrying and panicking and making her think something's wrong. I even out my features, manage to smile at her, and nod.

"Here we go, babe," I say. She seems to find my act convincing, because she fixes her big, beautiful blue eyes on me and nods, squeezing my arm even harder.

Time seems to have moved so slowly all day, but now that

the moment has arrived, everything kicks into overdrive. More nurses enter the room, and the doctor makes an appearance for the first time since approving the Pitocin.

The contractions keep coming, and then, suddenly, Pippa is screaming about needing to push. A nurse on the other side of her is coaching her through breathing, and the doctor is at the end of the birthing bed, giving us updates on what's happening. It seems like there are only seconds between contractions now, and Pippa listens to every instruction she's given. She's a warrior. She pushes, stops, breathes, pushes, stops, breathes. I rub her back, pull her hair back from where it's stuck to her forehead.

"One last push!" calls the doctor.

Just as the clock ticks over to Christmas Day, Pippa takes a couple of deep breaths and bears down, her face going deep red as she squeezes my hand, half-crushing my fingers in the process. There's a delighted murmur around the room, and then, a second later, the unmistakable cry of an infant fills the air.

My head snaps up from Pippa, and I see the doctor holding a tiny human attached to a long, purple-grey... tube. A baby. My baby. *Our* baby, I realize, as I look back to Pippa.

She is overcome with emotion, wearing a huge, exhausted smile with tears streaming down her cheeks. I lean down to kiss her and then wipe her tears away with my thumbs.

"Congratulations!" says the doctor. "A beautiful baby girl."

It's only when Pippa reaches up and swipes her thumb under my left eye that I realize I've shed a tear, too.

"Here she is," says the nurse, laying our cleaned up, bundled up daughter down on Pippa's chest.

There are some moments in life that you instantly know you'll remember forever. Seeing Pippa's face in the restaurant window was one. Looking down at my daughter and my future wife for the very first time is another. I feel a tear leak from my eye and swipe it away, leaning in to kiss the top of Pippa's head and get a better look at our daughter.

"She has your mouth," Pippa says, looking up at me. She's still a little flushed, but she's beaming a smile brighter than I've ever seen. She's never been so beautiful.

"Poor kid," I try to joke, but my voice wavers around the lump in my throat.

"We just need to take her for some checks," says a nurse, coming to Pippa's side after allowing us an appropriate amount of time to stare at her in dumbstruck wonder. "Perfectly routine. We won't be long."

Pippa lets our baby go, reluctantly, and I help her through the rest of her labor under the guidance of the most senior nurse. It isn't long before we're reunited with our little bundle, and we all move into a recovery ward.

Pippa and I are talking quietly while the baby sleeps on her chest, snickering about all the silly names we come up with, when the nurse comes into the room.

"Well, congratulations on your Christmas baby," she says. "First one of the day, this year. Any names yet?" she asks.

We both shake our heads.

"Not yet," says Pippa. "We didn't know we were going to have to name a person until earlier today."

"Ah, that's right," says the nurse. "Well, plenty of time. And you did so well, especially given the circumstances. You must be exhausted."

"She should sleep, right?" I say. I've asked Pippa to get some rest every few minutes since we got into the ward, but she keeps telling me she will "in a few minutes". She's as smitten with our baby girl as I am.

Pippa nudges me with her free elbow, and the nurse smiles.

"You should try to get some rest, yes," she tells Pippa, and I give my fiancée a smug little smile, earning me another dig in the ribs.

"It was an entirely uncomplicated birth, so the doctor says you can go home in the morning, after he's seen you, and spend Christmas at home. As long as you make sure to get a checkup in a few days."

"Great," says Pippa. Her voice crackles a little and her eyelids are droopy. The nurse takes that as her cue to leave, congratulating us again.

"Do you want me to tell Lexi and Dave to go to Lexi's place tomorrow instead of coming over to mine?" I ask Pippa, settling down in the chair beside her bed and running my finger over the back of our daughter's tiny little hand.

"No!" she says, far more forcefully than I expect. "No, let's all be together. I'd like that a lot. I mean, if that's alright with you?" Even in her exhausted state, she manages puppy eyes that would melt the devil's heart.

"Sure," I say. "But only on the condition that you promise me you'll rest now. And tomorrow if you need to." I look down at the baby. "Mind if I take her out to meet everyone?" I ask. "Or do you want me to wait?"

"Oh! No, I don't mind at all," she says. She hands our daughter over to me and I place her in the crib for a moment to give Pippa some attention. I lean down and pull the blankets up under her chin, and linger a slow kiss on her lips.

"You were a warrior, babe," I say.

She smiles at me, sleepily, and I take the baby out of the crib again and hold her in my arms, sitting in the chair until I hear Pippa's breathing even out to the low and steady rhythm of slumber. I kiss her on the forehead one last time, and then lean down to my gurgling daughter and whisper: "Come on, let's go meet some people."

Valerie and Lexi are both sleeping under Lexi's coat, and Dave is lounging across three chairs, scrolling through his phone with one eye half-open and the other closed. I look up at the clock and it's just after 1am.

"Hey!" says Dave, as soon as he spots me. He shoots to his

feet and stumbles a step or two, coming over with his gaze fixed on the bundle in my arms.

"Holy shit," he says. "I mean. Holy poop." I grin at him and chuckle.

"Isn't she the coolest thing?" I ask him.

"She?" he says. "Aww. Hey, Lex, look."

I look over, and Lexi has stirred from her sleep. She gives Valerie a nudge, and they're both over with us in seconds, all four of us looking down at this tiny bundle of perfection in my arms, all of us speaking in hushed voices.

"How's Pippa?" asks Valerie.

"Tired," I say. "She was amazing. She just fell asleep a few minutes ago. But she wanted you all to meet our daughter."

"Can I hold her?" Lexi asks, holding out her arms.

I oblige her, ever so carefully passing the little bundle off to Lexi and watching as my sister meets her niece for the very first time.

"Nothing but the very best designer everything for you, little one," she whispers, and Dave rolls his eyes exaggeratedly. He's still smiling, though, and the four of us are still staring at the baby as Lexi holds her.

"What's the plan for tomorrow?" asks Dave.

"Pippa would still like us all to have Christmas together," I tell him, and look around at Lexi and Valerie, who are nodding. "The nurse says they can both come home in the morning."

"I've called in a few favors," Lexi says. "Baby things and some bottles and formula, just in case. They'll be delivered tomorrow."

That's a huge relief. The prospect of having nothing at home for the baby had started to weigh on my mind.

"You're a champion, sis," I tell Lexi.

"Can I hold her?" asks Val, and Lexi hands the baby over.

"I'll go home tonight," says Val, looking down at my

daughter's peaceful, chubby little face. "Get Pip some clothes and toiletries."

"We can drop you on the way," says Dave. "And I can pick you up tomorrow, on the way back from getting Pippa and Aiden. And... her," he says, nodding to the baby. "I have snow tyres," he adds, proudly, and it's Lexi's turn to roll her eyes.

"That would be great. Thanks, Dave. You want to hold her?" Val asks, holding the baby out toward him.

"Nope!" says Dave, emphatically, both hands in the air. "No, thank you. I try not to hold anything too valuable or too fragile, and this is both." I smile at him, understanding his reluctance. He was the same when his sister's kids were born, but he's the most amazing uncle. Just needs them to grow a bit, first.

"Right," says Lexi, taking charge. "We'll get moving. You look exhausted. Get some rest."

I promise that I will, and I mean it. I'm wiped out. Val gently places my daughter back into my arms, and we arrange a time for Dave to pick us up in the morning. I give side-hugs to all of them, careful to keep my precious little load out of the way. They all congratulate me and head out, Dave dragging along the huge teddy behind him.

"Okay, little one," I whisper, when it's just me and my little girl left. "Let's get some rest."

By the time I get back to the ward, a nurse has laid out a fold-out bed for me, beside Pippa's. I lay the baby down in her clear plastic crib and just stand there for a while, watching both my girls sleeping peacefully. It strikes me, as I glance up and notice the unlit strip light above my head, that I feel more content than I've ever felt in my life. In a hospital, of all places. I'm exhausted, but I'm brimming with hope and love and happiness, and all because I agreed to be one wonderful, beautiful, brilliant girl's vacation fling.

Christmas Day, 2018

The baby is latched onto my left breast, suckling away, and Aiden and I are laughing and chatting about names while we wait for Dave to arrive. We've rejected at least two hundred already, some of them ridiculous and some that were at least somewhat appealing.

I feel remarkably well, all things considered. I'm a little sore when I stand up or sit down, and a little tired, but otherwise, I feel fine. The shock and terror of yesterday is gone, replaced by a deep feeling of awe every time I gaze at my daughter, or catch Aiden staring at her with a wistful look in his eye. I don't know what I would have done without him. Every time she woke up through the night, so did he—sitting with me, helping me, chatting to me as the baby quietly feeds.

"What was your grandmother's name?" Aiden asks, out of the blue. "The one who had the studio before you?"

Even the mention of the studio I might be losing can't bring me down today. I look up and smile at him, adoring

139

him for even thinking about naming our child after my grandmother. He's sitting on the chair looking a little crumpled in his day-old clothes, but still as gorgeous as ever.

"Jessica," I say, expecting him to dismiss the name out of hand.

"Jessica," he says thoughtfully, pursing his lips. He goes quiet.

When I look down, the baby has fallen asleep. I pull my gown back up, adjust the swaddle, and settle back on the bed.

"I like it," Aiden says.

"Really?" I ask, my brows lifting. It's my turn to look thoughtful as I think about it seriously for the first time, gazing down at the tiny bundle in my arms.

"Jessica," I say again, feeling the syllables on my tongue. I think about my grandmother, about her kind eyes and her generous heart, and a little smile finds my lips. She'd revel in this story. Her little Pip having a baby like this, the big, dramatic proposal beside the hospital bed. She was a sucker for a bit of drama.

"That's the one, isn't it?" he asks, leaning in. He places his hand on my back and gazes down at her with me. "Jessica."

I look to him, feeling a lump in my throat and tears welling in my eyes, and nod.

"Hi, baby Jessica," he whispers, with a broad grin.

I lean over and kiss his temple, barely able to believe that this, all of this, is mine. The man, the baby, the future that seems to stretch out before us, full of possibility. The fact that all of this came to be on Christmas Day is just the cherry on top.

"Ho, ho, ho!"

Dave's voice reaches the room a moment before he does. He practically bursts in, grinning from ear to ear and swinging a backpack from his shoulder.

"Merry Christmas!"

"Morning," I say, smiling and shaking my head at his entrance.

"How are mother and baby doing?" he asks. It's so strange that I am "mother" in that phrase now.

"Jessica," Aiden says, on his feet. He claps Dave on the back. "Her name's Jessica."

"Ahh, lovely," says Dave. "Well, let's get Ms. Pippa and Ms. Jessica home, shall we?" He places the bag down on the chair that Aiden just vacated.

"Clothes. Some for you, from Val, and some for Jessica, from Lexi. There's all sorts of boxes and crates being delivered this morning, so I don't know what the hell your sister's been up to," he says, looking to Aiden, "but I suspect that baby Jessica will want for nothing the rest of her days."

Aiden rolls his eyes, of course, and I laugh. I hand Jessica off to her dad and excuse myself to go shower and change. I feel so refreshed when I'm done, I find it hard to believe that I gave birth not even twelve hours ago.

The ride home is smooth and steady. I don't know where Dave found a baby seat on such short notice, or how the hell Lexi is managing to get things delivered on Christmas Day, for that matter, but I have no complaints about it. Aiden sits in the back with us, and Jessica sleeps the whole way. She doesn't even wake up when we stop to pick up Valerie, who steps into the car laden with bags and leans back between the front seats to give me a hug.

"Merry Christmas, Pip," she says, and proceeds to spend the rest of the journey staring at Jessica and giving me excited little smiles every time she stirs.

Dave was not wrong about the extent of Lexi's operation. When we walk in, she's on her hands and knees with a screwdriver, putting together a baby rocker. There's a mountain of diapers and formula tubs, a stroller, a bassinet, and a pile of wood and screws in the middle of the room that looks like it might eventually assemble into a crib.

141

"Lexi," I gasp, my eyes wide as I look around.

"Oh, hey, guys!" she says, gliding gracefully to her feet. She shoves the screwdriver into Dave's hand and comes over to hug me.

"Merry Christmas!" she says, looking down at Jessica, and waves a hand, as though dismissing all the effort she's obviously been to. "We ran a feature on a little mom-and-pop baby store last year that pushed them national. Lisa—that's the owner, lovely woman—was more than happy to help out."

"Thank you so, so much, Lexi," I say, breathlessly. I'd been worried about how we were going to get everything we'd need during the holiday period. The relief I feel at seeing everything all laid out is immeasurable.

"Don't mention it," says Lexi. "Get yourself comfortable. Aiden and I are cooking later, but you rest as much as you need. Can I get you a drink? A snack?"

"I'll do that," says Aiden. "Thanks, Lex."

Lexi turns to Dave, who's still standing in the same spot, holding the screwdriver, and gives him a playful shove. Together, they go back to assembling the baby furniture, while Aiden goes to the kitchen to make us all some brunch, and Valerie comes with me—clearly angling for another chance to hold the baby. I oblige her, and take the opportunity to finally dig my phone, which I haven't set eyes on since yesterday, out of my bag. It's entirely dead.

As soon as I connect the charger and switch it on, it starts going haywire, buzzing and beeping.

"Ohhhh. Yeah," says Val, looking sheepish. "Sorry, should have told you right away. Your mom called last night. She was worried because she couldn't get through to you. I uh... told her about the baby. But I said everything was fine," she adds, hurriedly.

"I have one hundred and sixty-three missed calls," I say, staring at the phone now that it's finally settled down. "And twenty-seven voicemails. And," I say, looking up to Val with an expression of amazement on my face, "five text messages."

"She *texted*?!" asks Val, looking as shocked as me.

My mother is not a texter. She only has a smartphone because it came with her plan. If she could get a cell that looks and acts like a rotary dial, she definitely would.

I'm still staring at the phone in disbelief when it starts vibrating and ringing, and I hurry to answer it before it wakes Jessica.

"Hi, Mom," I say, waiting for the onslaught.

"Oh, thank GOD!" she cries through the earpiece. "Phillippa, what on earth..." I cringe a little, my shoulder rising into it, but then her voice evens out and, a little breathlessly, she asks "Are you alright? What happened? Do you want me to come home?"

I assure her that I'm fine. I tell her briefly about Aiden and about the baby, that I'm engaged, and that she has a granddaughter now. She sounds emotional about it all, but she loses it completely when I tell he we've named our daughter after her mother. I manage to convince her to enjoy the rest of her once-in-a-lifetime Christmas vacation to Italy, and tell her I'll see her when they get back.

My dad, who's been getting all the details squawked at him across a hotel room, sounds much calmer when he comes on the line.

"You're alright, love?" he asks, in his usual placid, sensible tone.

"Yes, Dad," I tell him. I do wish they were here to meet Jessica, but they'll be back in only a couple of weeks, and it's probably for the best that they're away. My mother's fussing would probably drive me mad. At least this way, I have some time to settle and get used to being a mom, myself. Get used to being a part of my new little family.

"Got everything you need?" Dad asks.

"Yes, Dad."

"Alright. Well call us if there's anything *else* you need. Give little Jessica a cuddle from me, and we'll see you when we're back. And I'll meet this man of yours and see what he's all about."

"Dad," I say, and the roll of my eyes is in my voice.

"Love you, kiddo," he says, chuckling.

"Love you, too," I say, and hit the button to end the call.

I spend the rest of the day switching between the master bedroom and the sitting room in Aiden's huge, beautiful apartment. I nap when I need to and take breaks to feed Jessica, and enjoy everyone's company. Despite how relatively little everyone knows each other, there's a familiar warmth that makes me just *know* that everything is going to work out.

Brunch is delicious, and so is dinner. Lexi keeps us all entertained with stories about celebrities and singers and their antics, Dave keeps us entertained with embarrassing tales from Aiden and Lexi's childhoods, and Val, who has fit right into the group, makes us all roar with laughter by regaling us with her first impressions of Aiden as a slave-driving bore at work.

"I was nervous!" Aiden protests, his arm draped around my shoulders, but Dave takes the opportunity to rib him, anyway.

A couple of hours after dinner, while Jessica is snoozing away in the rocker and the others have decided to tackle the dishes, Lexi comes over and sits beside me.

"Got a minute?" she asks.

"Sure," I say. "She's sound asleep, anyway."

"She's adorable," Lexi says, looking down to Jessica. "Best Christmas present I ever had."

I'm suddenly grinning, remembering the trouble Aiden was having, trying to find a suitably sentimental gift for Lexi. It doesn't get much better than meeting your first niece on Christmas Day.

"I just wanted to chat with you about your studio," she says. The familiar niggle of worry creeps in, and I frown involuntarily.

"There's nothing I can do about it," I say. "Aiden said—"

"Legally," Lexi interjects. "There's nothing you can do about it *legally*. But I called Mr. Ling Jr. to speak to him about the feature we're doing on you." She has the humility to look a little embarrassed as she goes on. "Turns out, Mr. Ling Jr. has a semi-successful re-selling business, and that's worth more to him than a one-time windfall from selling the studio, or a slightly higher rent."

"What are you getting at?" I ask her. I can feel myself leaning forward a little, afraid to believe where I think she's going with this.

"Well, he's not too keen on being written into your article as the evil landlord threatening your creative space," she says, giving me a meaningful look.

I blink at her. For a moment, I feel bad for Mr. Ling Jr.— and then I remember that he was about to turf me out without a second thought. He didn't even call me to let me know his father had died.

"Oh, Lexi," I say, leaning into her and giving her a joyous hug. "I can't thank you enough. You've been so good to me."

"Don't mention it," she says, giving me a squeeze back. "We're family."

We do play charades in the end, though the team of Lexi and Dave prove unbeatable. And when everyone is full of food and wine and cheer, and have said their good-nights, Aiden and I retire to bed together, for the first time since the cabin.

Standing in the en suite beside him while we brush our teeth is the strangest and yet the most natural thing in the world. He looks at me and waggles his brows with white foam all around his mouth, and I laugh. Somehow, I manage to inhale a fleck of toothpaste, and the burning mint at the back of my throat makes me choke and cough, and spray toothpaste all over the huge mirror that extends right across the wall.

When I look up at Aiden, he's grinning broadly, watching me.

"Go to bed, you shambles," he laughs, wiping his mouth. He leans down and kisses me on the top of the head. "I'll clean up."

Five minutes later, we're in bed. Jessica is gurgling away peacefully in a sleeper beside us, and I'm laying beside Aiden, tucked into his side with my arm draped across his chest. His fingers smooth their way through my hair, rhythmically, in the darkness, and his broad chest rises and falls slowly.

"Pip?" he says, sleepily.

"Mmm?"

"I love you."

I smile, even though he can't see me. I'm warm and comfortable and content, full of hope and happiness. I run my forefinger over the band of the too-big engagement ring that's found its home on my thumb.

"I love you, too," I say.

"Both of you," he says.

"Same."

A few minutes later, his hand stills on my head and his breathing deepens as he falls asleep. I'm not quite tired enough yet, having napped through the day, so I lay there, awake, enjoying the warmth of his body and the combined rhythm of my fiance's and my daughter's breathing as they slumber.

This is home, I realize. And I realize that, although I couldn't admit it to myself at the time, I had that same feeling when I lay beside Aiden in the cabin all those months ago, in a different world, a different time, a different place. *He* is home.

When I gaze at the window, I can see the little green light

of the baby monitor reflected back at me, dancing over the scene outside. It's close to midnight, and the moon is out, an almost-perfect circle suspended high over the skyscrapers and rooftops below, its light glittering across the thick blanket of snow that covers them, pillowy and undisturbed.

EPILOGUE

PIPPA

Valentine's Day, 2019

"Oh, love," says my mother, looking at me tearfully, dabbing at the corners of her eyes with a little handkerchief. "You look absolutely beautiful."

She's holding Jessica in her arms, rocking her back and forth as the baby sleeps, as oblivious as she's been all morning to all the surrounding commotion. I smile at my mother and lean in to kiss her cheek, and when I pull back, she dabs at her eyes again before heading into the venue.

I have to admit that I do feel good. It turns out that nine months of the *Eat, Pray, Love* lifestyle actually does do wonders for your body. You just don't notice if you happen to be unwittingly pregnant at the same time.

The A-line dress I'm wearing is made of ivory silk charmeuse and swishes around my ankles every time I take a step. It's beautifully cut and fitted, thanks to a celebrity designer that Lexi knows, and it has intricate embroidery around the hem that matches the long, silk-lace sleeves.

"Almost time, Poppet," says my dad, arriving at my side,

fiddling with the flower on his lapel. "Not too late to back out, you know."

This is typical humor from my dad, and I just roll my eyes at him as I bat his hand away and help him to straighten out the flower. He loved Aiden the moment he met him on New Year's Day. I'm pretty sure he'd divorce my mother and marry Aiden just to get him in the family if I backed out now.

"Two minutes!" says Lexi, excitedly, as she half-skips out of the hall, giving an excited little clap. She is drop-dead gorgeous in the deep burgundy gown she's wearing, with her blond hair swept up on her head. Valerie is hot on her heels, looking just as stunning in a matching gown that's dark navy, and they both have a gold sash around their waist.

"Nervous?" asks Val.

"Nah," I say, finally getting Dad's flower straight. "Why would I be? You two have to go first."

They laugh, but the truth is that after giving birth with only a few hours notice, and spending the past seven weeks adjusting to motherhood and to life with Aiden in the middle of the city, this feels like a cakewalk. There's not a single doubt in my mind about whether I'm doing the right thing. Aiden has been the best partner a woman could ask for, and the best father a girl could wish for.

Music begins to seep out of the hall. Val hands me my bouquet of ivory, burgundy and navy roses, full of winter sprigs, and gives me a quick air-kiss to avoid spoiling my makeup. Lexi steals a hug, and then, with a mutual nod, they both walk purposefully into the hall together. My dad offers me the crook of his left elbow and gives me a reassuring wink, and before I know it the music has changed to Wagner's Bridal chorus. It's our turn. The double doors in front of us open wide, and we start walking slowly down the makeshift aisle.

The hall of Driscoll's resort is nothing like I remembered. The chairs are clothed in beautiful ivory covers and decorated with gold ribbons, flowers matching mine adorn the ends of the rows, and the wooden walls are draped beautifully with rich fabrics.

When I look to the front of the hall, I see Aiden standing there, devilishly handsome in his pale, smoky gray suit, decorated with a burgundy cravat, grinning at me. I smile at him, and, for good measure, when I approach him closer and the guests are all behind me, I bite at my bottom lip. He narrows his eyes at me, and I dip my head to suppress a chuckle.

The past seven weeks have been an exercise in patience, for both of us. Six weeks were obligatory abstinence, on doctor's orders, and then we decided to abstain a little longer, until our wedding night. Well, okay—we didn't strictly "decide" that. Aiden bet me I wouldn't be able to resist him, and I took it as a challenge. Consequently, he's spent the last week trying to rile me; kissing my neck then feigning disinterest, unveiling his ridiculously hot body slowly before getting into bed and pulling me against him while his erection presses against my back. It almost worked, one night, when a make-out session during Jessica's nap got particularly heavy, but a hundred dollars is a hundred dollars. And a stubborn streak is a stubborn streak.

The service goes smoothly throughout. Having spent the last seven weeks caring for a needy newborn, we've opted to forego writing our own vows. We each repeat after the officiant, looking into each other's eyes, holding each other's hands. It feels like a dream, as I listen to him recite my full name and vow all of the evers and every one of the afters.

The officiant turns to the guests and asks: "If anyone can show just cause why this couple cannot lawfully be joined together in matrimony, let them speak now or forever hold their peace," and the obligatory awkward silence follows. I stare up at Aiden, my eyes twinkling with humor. And then Jessica decides to gurgle loudly into the silence. I laugh, along with my almost-husband and the entire congregation.

"You may kiss the bride," says the officiant, finally. Aiden leans down, one hand on my waist and the other on the back of my neck. His lips touch mine and I feel a jolt of joy in my tummy, fluttering around wildly. Our guests clap and cheer, and when they—and I—realize he's not stopping, everyone laughs. Aiden slips his hand a little further around my waist, holding me tight and tipping me back until I have to break the kiss to laugh, myself. He's grinning when I look up at him, his eyes glittering.

"Hello, wife," he says. I bite my bottom lip, smiling, and he kisses me again, deeper, before returning me to my feet.

The food they serve at the reception in Driscoll's bar is delicious. There's bubbly on arrival, canapes while we wait, then a six-course meal that I can hear everyone talking about enthusiastically, long after the dessert plates have been cleared away. Aiden's parents chat to me throughout; his mother is particularly interested in how Jessica is getting on, who did my hair, and if I know whether Lexi is dating anyone at the moment.

The speeches are hilarious and heartwarming in equal measure. Aiden's dad gives me a wonderful welcome into the family. Aiden has everyone near tears when he talks about how lucky he is and how beautiful I am, and about the unexpected Christmas miracle that is our daughter. My dad issues just enough threats in Aiden's direction to be funny, but not overbearing. And Dave has everyone rolling in their seats with stories about Aiden's childhood trips to the resort.

The band strikes up for the first dance, and Aiden and I take our positions. We slow dance around the floor to a chorus of claps and camera flashes from our guests. Aiden sweeps me around as though I weighed no more than a feather, and leans down to whisper in my ear.

"You're beautiful in that dress," he says.

I look up to him and smile.

"But I bet you'll be more beautiful out of it, later."

I feel my cheeks flush, and I chuckle, realising with some surprise that I'm *nervous*.

"Oh, beautiful, delicious Pip," Aiden says beside my ear, his breath hot on my neck. He takes my waist a little more firmly in his grip and pulls me closer. "Did you really think you won our little game?" he asks.

I look up and he's grinning down at me devilishly, looking like he might throw me over his shoulder and cart me off any second. I realize what he's been doing for the last week:, winding me up, bringing me to the verge of giving up on my own stubbornness, then stopping at the last second, making me anticipate our wedding night more and more with every passing day. Without even thinking about it, I bite my lower lip in response, and his eyes zoom in on my mouth, his jaw clenching visibly with pure lust.

"We're leaving in twenty minutes," he says, as the first dance draw to a close. He pulls me close, one strong arm around my waist while the other hand cups the back of my head and he probes my mouth with his tongue. I can hear our guests cheering, but I'm so dizzy with need for my new husband that they sound distant and muffled. "So be ready."

I have to take a moment to compose myself when we're off the dancefloor, then I excuse myself to go and speak to my mother. She's about to retire, too, with Jessica. I shower my daughter with kisses and cuddles around her ear protectors, Aiden comes over to do the same, and then we wave them off.

"Ready?" asks Aiden, when they're gone. Everyone else is distracted on the dancefloor, boogying away to an upbeat medley of love songs.

I press my lips together and nod. Without another word, he takes my hand and sweeps me away from the hall.

AIDEN

I carry my wife over the threshold into the cabin—the very same cabin we spent that wonderful first week in, almost a year ago—kissing her and enjoying her giggles as she holds tight around my neck. As soon as we're inside, I stop in my tracks. Lexi and Dave have outdone themselves.

"Wow," says Pippa, looking around the room. I place her down, gently, and spare a moment to take it all in.

The curtains have been drawn, and little jars with candles inside them glitter all around the room. The fire is roaring away, crackling and popping occasionally, and pillows and blankets have been draped artfully over the couches. Atop the table in the middle of the room sits a large bucket full of ice, with a bottle of fine champagne sticking out of it and two glasses sitting beside it, a fresh strawberry in the bottom of each one.

"No kidding," I say to Pippa, giving her hand a squeeze and smiling at her.

"So... I guess we're both about ready to turn in for the night?" she asks, nonchalantly.

I turn to look at her, narrowing my eyes as I see hers sparkling with amusement.

Her sense of humor was one of the first things I liked about her when we met. I laughed until my gut ached that first week, but at the time I thought it was just a frivolous thing, shallow and unimportant. Now that we've been together a little longer, moved in together, had a baby together, all at the sort of breakneck speed that would have shattered many couples, I realize it's a fundamental part of her. It's like glue, holding us together, making everything just that little bit easier. Life with her isn't just pleasant - it's *fun*.

I lean down beside her and brush her hair back, away from her neck. My lips find the shell of her ear and brush her skin, ever so gently. I place the softest kiss I can manage against the side of her neck, another against her jawline, and another at the very corner of her beautiful mouth. She stares up at me with her huge, blue eyes, and I run my thumb across her lower lip.

"Do *you* want to turn in?" I ask.

She swallows, bites her bottom lip at the spot I've just touched, and shakes her head.

I scoop her up again, carrying her over to the bedroom, and nearly kick the door off its hinges in my need to have her again. Inside, there are more candles dotted around the room, throwing dancing light against the walls, and the bed is strewn with rose petals.

"Pretty," she says, as I place her down.

"I've seen prettier," I tell her, looking into her deep blue eyes. I lower myself down on top of her and take her mouth in a deep, passionate kiss.

There's eight long weeks' worth of desire for her pent up inside me. Every time she's laughed or smiled, every time she's taken care of our daughter without complaint in the wee hours, or sat in her makeshift office, making sketches or emailing clients; pretty much every time I've looked at her, I've wanted to be inside her again. The last week has been particularly difficult, knowing that I could probably win our silly competition, but wanting to save it all for tonight. My length is straining hard against my pants, pressing against her thigh as she lets out a soft moan into my mouth.

"You're sure you're ready?" I whisper.

She grabs my cravat and wrenches me back down, kissing me eagerly and nodding. I don't need any more encouragement than that.

Reaching down, I pull up her lovely gown, drape by drape, until it's bunched around her waist.

"Filthy," I groan against her lips, when I realize she has no underwear. It means she's had no underwear on all day, and the thought drives me wild.

"It's just because I didn't want to h—"

I swallow her excuse with another kiss and reach down to where her hands are already trying to find my zipper.

"Shall I be gentle with you, Mrs. Coleman?" I ask, undoing my belt. She's squeezing at my bulge with her hand, and I'm having trouble restraining myself. But restrain myself I must, and I will, if she needs me to. We have our entire lives to do this. Every single day.

She finds my zipper and peels it down, popping the clasp of my pants a moment later. I feel her hand close around my cock and a loud, satisfied groan escapes me.

"No," she whispers, shaking her head.

She strokes me with a firm grip, and I reach down and wrench down the front of her dress. Her breasts spill forth and I dip my head, drawing one of her hardened nipples into my mouth and sucking gently.

"Are you sure?" I ask, thrusting myself through her fist with short, barely restrained snaps of my hips. She must surely be able to feel the pent up tension running through me.

Parting her thighs wider, she wraps her legs around my waist and releases my length, pulling me toward her.

"Fuck your wife," she whispers, and her words murder my restraint.

I line up and look down at her, wanting to sink right into her, but aware enough of her wellbeing to hold back a little. I feel the warmth and wetness as I start to push, gently, and watch her face for any signs of pain or discomfort.

It's a bad idea. The way her eyes roll as I press into her drives me wild. A shudder begins with the clenching of my balls and travels all the way through my body, and I lean down into her, snapping my hips forward until I'm buried to my sack, my mouth on hers, straining to hold still as she gasps and squeezes her legs tighter around my waist.

I reach down between her legs to find that sensitive little bundle of nerve endings that will be her undoing, and start to roll my thumb in a circle. I feel her relax underneath me, her brows lifting as she starts to respond, arching her back in invitation.

No longer able to restrain myself, I begin to roll my hips, rhythmically, slowly at first, but not for long. I thrust my hips, over and over, watching the tiny changes in her face, watching her cheeks turn a pretty pink and her chest a deep red. I'm in danger of spilling over, so I slow down, focus all my attention on her, circling my thumb around at that same, steady pace and matching it with my hips.

She looks so beautiful there, so obscenely beautiful, laid back on the bed with her breasts bared and her dress hiked up around her waist, her legs open, her head thrust back. She gasps huge, desperate gasps of air, her hands in the blankets, gripping at rich cotton and pretty rose petals. She takes a particularly large gasp of air and holds it, and I know exactly what's coming.

As soon as I hear the first peep of her moan and feel the clench around my length, I grab her hips and pull her toward me, leaning down again and slamming my hips forward, faster, harder, prolonging her orgasm while I chase down my own. She is moaning loudly in my ear, renewed pleasure ringing out of her with every snap of my hips. My heart is thundering in my chest, my thighs are aching from the force I'm putting into every thrust, and then... release. My head explodes into a cacophony of pleasure, and I spill inside her, pressing, desperately, pushing as deeply into her as I possibly can. Breathless, heaving huge gulps of air while she twitches underneath me, I still.

Looking down, I see her lips formed into one of her secret little smiles, and lean down to peck a panting kiss to her mouth.

"I love you, Mrs. Coleman," I tell her, as I ease myself off her and roll onto my back, pulling her into my side. She wriggles into me, draping her arm across my chest, and her eyes are satisfied, glittering little stars.

"I love you, too, Mr. Coleman," she says, and I am complete.

DELETED CHAPTER

If you enjoyed Pippa and Aiden's journey to their Happy Ever After and you just can't get enough, sign up to my mailing list at www.harmonyknight.com to read about the very first time they met.

Oh, and if you loved Lexi and Dave as much as I did, keep an eye out for news about them, coming soon!

Love and Rockets,

Harmony

xoxo

ABOUT THE AUTHOR

Harmony Knight is an emerging romance author. Born and raised in an ex-mining village in South Wales (UK), where the only amenity was a post office and the only escape a twice-daily bus, she became an avid reader and book-lover from a very young age. After kissing her fair share of frogs, she found her prince and moved across the Irish Sea, from the land of song and dragons to the Emerald Isle, where she now lives with her family. She writes the books she loves to read, full of competent heroines and the caring alpha men who have to have them, and she hopes you'll love to read them, too!

For news and updates, check out her website at www.harmonyknight.com.

This is Harmony's debut novel.